r
c
v

c
is
sc

t
7.
s

w
w
al
th

y
pi
w,
sto
adu

Heads You Win, Tails I Lose

Also by Isabelle Holland

Heads You Win, Tails I Lose

a novel by ISABELLE HOLLAND

J. B. LIPPINCOTT COMPANY

Philadelphia and New York

U.S. Library of Congress Cataloging in Publication Data

Holland, Isabelle.
  Heads you win, tails I lose.

  SUMMARY: A young girl embarks unknowingly on a dangerous
regime to lose weight while her parents are absorbed in marital difficulties.
  [1. Family problems—Fiction] I. Title.
PZ7.H7083He   [Fic]   73-5811
ISBN 0-397-31380-2

One

My life changed forever that autumn day shortly after school started, although I didn't know it at the time. All I knew was that Ted MacDonald, generally known as Tremendous Teddy and the love of my life since I was nine, was rejecting me, and my heart was broken.

Of course, I should never have asked Teddy how he thought I rated generally, no matter how much reassurance I needed. But I did.

After a lick of his chocolate, chocolate chip ice cream cone and a long look, he delivered judgment: "You're too fat. Otherwise, I guess, you're all right. Face, not bad. Personality, okay."

Whatever I expected, or more likely hoped for, the

shock of his words was like a kick. "Your generosity is over-whelming," I said sarcastically, to keep from crying.

"You asked me." His slate blue eyes watched me over his towering cone. He took another lick. I could feel the taste of it all the way down my gullet.

"Brains?" I asked, not because I thought I didn't have any—I've been an A student since I can remember—but more to see how they rated among Teddy's priorities for a woman. I found out.

"You ought to know the answer to that, so why are you asking me? You get straight A's, don't you? If you want to be a hot women's libber I suppose that's important."

I didn't particularly want to be a hot women's libber. I didn't even particularly want to be an A student. What I have wanted since I was nine and he moved next door is to be the love of Ted MacDonald's life, and in the six years since then, I have tried just about everything: I've done his homework, sat up all night with his dog when it was run over (Ted went sound asleep while I stayed awake to force-feed water from an eyedropper into Maggie every hour), held up the target in a darts contest for him when it came unglued and fell off the wall, played straight man to the great comedian when he found himself with a banana peel and an audience and acted as a willing one-girl laboratory when he wanted to find out if one of his home-concocted chemistry experiments was poisonous. I've been sat on, bitten, rolled over and set fire to (that was accidental; Teddy found some odd-looking matches and said I should have the first strike: ladies first and all that), all towards the one end of making Teddy realize that I was the woman with whom he would choose to walk, hand in hand, into the sunset, with the music from *Love Story* playing in the background.

And then, a month ago, he fell in love with Claire Reynolds, and the crash could be heard all over Westchester. Suddenly Teddy, the pasha of the neighborhood who had graciously allowed me to risk life and limb just for the privilege of staying around him, started fixing Claire's car, falling off his training diet so he could lounge around Ye Olde Coffee Shoppe (known as The Shoppey) with her, turning up at drama club meetings instead of going out for track and, generally, forgetting that I was alive.

Why?

Shamed and heartbroken, I was weak enough to confide my misery to Mother, and she lost no time in letting me have her version of the answer. "A good-looking boy like Teddy, who can have any girl he wants, usually goes for a little slip of a thing like Claire: slender, feminine, pretty. And it's not that I haven't tried to help you with your appearance. I gave you that whole series for teen-age grooming at that salon in New York and you never went after the first time. You have a very pr—well, pretty enough face, lovely skin. If you'd just go on a *diet*."

So, in addition to the agonies of unrequited love, I had given Mother her cue to embark once again on her current favorite topic: my losing weight. It's a crusade she's been waging for the last year or so and remains a steady favorite while other enthusiasms come and go.

Mother is nothing if not with it. In an unfortunate moment at dinner once, she entangled herself in a phrase that went something like, "those of us who try to mold the avant-garde of public opinion."

I saw Father's eyebrows twitch. "I think you have something slightly mixed there," he said.

"You know what I mean," she said a little haughtily.

"I should rather describe you as a dedicated follower," Father replied, and they were off on yet another skirmish in the Hammond Wars, which probably started as they marched down the aisle of that big church in New York, and by this time, if they had received proper documentation, would exceed Caesar's commentaries.

As usual, on that occasion Mother ended up getting the worst of the battle of tongues. Father was smarter, quicker and better at keeping his cool. Mother, who could never seem to remember this, had launched on her latest enthusiasm, women's liberation, male exploitation over centuries and her need to assert her rights as a first-class citizen.

Father said, "If that means you'll be equally responsible for your bills and parking tickets, I'll endorse the whole movement, no questions asked."

That, Mother said, was a typically male chauvinist statement and a clear example of why their marriage had never been a success.

"I wish you'd told me sooner that it was a failure," Father said. "Think of all the time I've been wasting when I could have been training someone else for the role."

"Not that you haven't—" Mother started, and then shut up. Father's amused look iced over.

There was a silence while they bottled up their fight over Father's girl friend in New York that they thought I didn't know about. I sat there eating my weight-control dinner of string beans, broccoli and chicken and drinking my skim milk and trying to concentrate on how funny it all was, all three of us knowing about Father's secretary and the nights he had to spend in town working, and them wanting to have another fight about her, only not doing so because they think I don't know. I wouldn't have to tell anyone my age how much I know about those fights, having heard three or four from behind the closed doors of Father's study or their bedroom. The rooms are not soundproofed, and while Father's voice stays even and it's sometimes hard to hear his side, Mother's, which is pretty carrying anyway, goes soaring up whenever she gets excited, which is about half the time, and all the time when they're arguing. I used to listen at the doors when I was younger. That was the way I learned that the only reason they're staying together is because of me. Now I don't bother. I know everything they're going to say anyway, because they've said it all before.

Mother's kind of a joke around our Westchester suburb. Whatever the newest movement or intellectual fashion is, she's out there leading it. Father once acidly commented that if cannibalism ever returned he and I had better pack fast, because there was nothing Mother liked better than setting an example. Which was cruel as well as funny. But Father can be cruel.

Once, when I was about seven and attending a progressive experimental elementary school where they managed to find a prize for practically every girl and boy, so all the parents would be happy and everybody's identity made secure, I was awarded the prize for doing the best work considering the length of time I had been out with measles and mumps. This was long before my all-A's period and I was terribly excited about it because I'd never had a prize before. I was jumping around at home the night of the prize-giving when Father came home. If I hadn't been so full of myself I would have noticed that his limp was pronounced and taken warning. It was always a sure sign he'd had a bad day. But I didn't. And when I told him about my prize and Mother added that he'd have to skip his drink (she'd had her two or so) and hurry through dinner to get to the ceremony, he lashed out with one of his quiet savageries.

"You realize, Melissa, that your prize is simply some kind of consolation gift to you for making the poorest showing. For being the class dunce. That's how they keep reluctant and reactionary taxpayers happy."

Even while I sobbed hysterically I knew that it was more a slap at Mother than at me. Father wanted me to go to the regular old-fashioned elementary school. But Mother was in what was afterward referred to as her Zelda Fitzgerald phase and for some reason that meant a progressive school.

So, after she had all but picked me up with a sponge and clasped me to her still-boyish bosom smelling deliciously of Joy perfume (seventy-five dollars an ounce), she and Father had one of their more heroic battles, Mother's drama-school-trained voice rising to what should have been the third gallery and Father getting whiter and more silent as he dragged his leg back and forth across the room. Instead of admitting that what he'd said was an abomination, a piece of humble pie-swallowing that (I realized long afterward) Mother was making more impossible with every accusatory word, he tried to justify it. He said that I was (a) stupid and (b) unattractive, and thus would be a disgrace to him up there on the platform. Father liked little slips of a girl, too.

That's why he married one. You'd think, at that point, that I should have submitted to my natural fate and joined the circus. Actually, the facts were not that gruesome. At seven I was (there was no denying it) tubby.

Now, at fifteen, I'm still tubby, but the tub is bigger, of course, since I'm older. There's more, so to speak, square footage. But it hasn't impeded me at all. I've always been sort of a tomboy; I can fly over the horse at gym with the best and am on the junior swimming team. I'm not exactly the girl star track runner, but I'm on the field hockey team, too, and even though Claire, my greatest enemy, once said that the reason for my success lay in everybody's fear that I would run into them (that witticism went around the school in about ten minutes), it's not true. I could lose ten pounds. Or fifteen. That is, theoretically. Mother says twenty. But then Mother's formula for success is getting into a size eight at forty. Since she passed that magic marker a year or two ago and even wears a size seven, you can see she has achieved it. Which just makes it more difficult for me. And now that Mother wears nothing but jeans and rib-hugging sweaters and pants suits she's getting, if anything, thinner.

Not long ago, as they were setting out for a cocktail party given by one of Father's law partners and Mother came downstairs in a sleek black pants suit, looking like one of the Hell's Angels gang, Father said, "It almost kills me to have to suggest that you buy some new clothes—but don't you have anything else? I realize you look upon the Randalls as doltish relics of the *ancien régime,* but since it's their house and their party, couldn't you cater to them just a little?"

Father, I need hardly say, was in a charcoal gray suit, striped tie and white shirt. His dark hair, apart from streaks

of gray, is exactly the way it's been since he came out of the
Air Force sixteen years ago after the crash that shattered his
leg.

Mother paused halfway down the stairs. "I can't imagine why you don't go in a periwig and satin knee breeches
like your true spiritual counterpart, Louis XIV, or your
other one, George III."

"If I thought it would get you back into skirts, I might.
This is a conservative suburb and I prefer not to be thought
of as consorting with adolescent boys, which is exactly what
you look like."

Sally, one of my best friends, assures me that most of
the families in this upper affluent suburb an hour from New
York have about the same degree of togetherness, one way
or another, as mine. Those that seem to have a chummier at-
mosphere are the ones that scratched the first effort, got di-
vorced and started all over. Theirs are the kids who are always going off to spend holidays or weekends with their
other set of parents, and next to envying the girls with no
weight problem, I envy them. For one thing, they can—and
do—play off one set of parents against the other. I know one
girl who, having achieved real skill at this, has collected
thirty-five cashmere sweaters, having decided that year that
she was going in for cashmere.

But to get back to Ted. I hate to be so direly corny,
but in the best American myth/Andy Hardy tradition, he's
the boy next door. I fell in love with him the first day I saw
him, the day the MacDonalds moved in. I was nine. He was
ten.

The movers were lugging in furniture and his parents

had disappeared into the house. I was running slowly around in a small circle repeating to myself:

> *a ab absque coram de*
> *pallum cum* and *ex* and *e* . . .

to make a spell. That was my witch phase and I was making a spell (a) to be thinner, (b) that my father's leg would get well and he'd be in a better humor and (c) that Mother would stop causing me a lot of embarrassment by coming to school to make sure that I was being allowed to express myself freely.

I had carefully kept my attention off the goings-on next door because one of the rules about the spell was that if you stopped before you finished or even allowed your attention to waver for as much as a second the spell wouldn't work, and you couldn't even try it again for a week, or everything you were doing the spell *for* would come out backward. That is, I'd get fatter, Father's leg would get worse, if that was at all possible, and still stay on his body, and Mother would drop into school every day instead of every other day.

Of all those horrors the last was the worst. Vivid in my mind was the most recent visit, Mother's voice rising clearly over the howls of Betty Armstrong whom I had just punched in the midriff: "But Miss Peabody, to punish Melissa for simply expressing her natural hostility to being presented with an unacceptable self-image by an antagonistic peer—"

"Melissa can't go around punching people. That's why

she's being punished," Miss Peabody said. She was as old-fashioned as her Girl Guide shoes.

Mother's sky blue eyes flashed. "Surely an appropriate response ought to include the primary aggressor agent—who was Betty."

"As soon as Betty stops howling she'll be given extra arithmetic, too."

"I really don't think arithmetic is cognitively related in any significant psychosocietal dynamic with interpersonal conflict."

Even in the midst of my rage I could see Miss Peabody's patience was running out. She obviously didn't appreciate the hard work Mother had put into reading educational manuals.

"I'd make them copy St. Paul's letter on charity if I didn't think the Supreme Court would descend in a body, gowns fluttering."

"Surely that would be violating the constitutional edict on separation of Church and State."

"You don't have to tell me. Mrs. Hammond, do you think you could leave this to me?"

Mother positively glowed with indignation. "You can hardly have read the Education Board's last paper on the enlightened response in the classroom to peer interchange."

"I never read their papers," Miss Peabody said. "Melissa, get on with your work. Betty, if you don't stop howling and upsetting the entire class I'll take you to the principal."

"She called me a fat pig," I said furiously.

Betty's howls stopped. "Cow," she corrected, and

started up again. Before either Mother or Miss Peabody could move I whacked her again.

"They should have a dialogue," Mother shrieked above the din.

"This *is* a dialogue—of a kind," Miss Peabody yelled back, frog-marching both Betty and me to the door.

That was, of course, after I had, at Father's insistence, transferred to the regular nonexperimental school. Anyway, the class never let me forget it. In addition to being "fatty," I was "Mother's pet." It was too much. That was why I was making the spell.

As I chugged around I saw this handsome blond boy staring at me from about ten feet away. But I would not allow myself to be distracted. Then he spoke up.

"Do you always run around talking to yourself?"

"Sine tenus pro and *prae,"* I said loudly, jogging along.

"They'll take you away in a padded wagon," he said. He watched me for a minute. "You're not exactly the athletic type."

"Add *super subter sub* and *in,"* I went on loudly. He must not be allowed to break in on my spell.

"That's Latin," he said with what Mother would now call male chauvinist obviousness. "Did you know your stomach jiggles up and down when you run?"

"WHEN STATE NOT MOTION 'TIS THEY MEAN," I yelled, finishing the spell. Then I jogged over to him and landed a beauty in his eye. But it was not as hard as I originally intended, because just before my fist connected I saw him properly and my heart gave a great thud. He was BEAUTIFUL. And I fell in love.

That was six years ago, and at fifteen I was still in love. Much good it did me. My father once described Teddy as the triumph of matter over any reliable evidence of mind, and although I didn't speak to Father for several days after he made that crack, every now and then I had a sinking feeling it might be true.

I tried hard to remember this when Teddy told me I was fat. But it still made me very cast down, and remembering that Claire, my enemy, was his girl didn't help either.

Teddy finished his ice cream cone and wiped his fingers on his jeans. Keats said that a thing of beauty was a joy forever. Its loveliness increaseth. Well, Teddy was far from a joy forever. Right up there with my parents, he was the chief pain in my life. But the poet was on target about the rest. His loveliness increased constantly. It was depressing.

At sixteen Teddy was about five foot eleven and still going up. All the youthful horrors—ganZliness, Adam's apple and acne—had bypassed him. His tanned skin was slightly freckled but smooth as a peach. His wavy chestnut hair was shiny. His muscles bulged romantically. Beautiful fantasies of feeling that biceps curving into my back as he stole his arm around me floated before my inner eye. That was when I made my terrible mistake and my life turned sour. "You do like me, don't you, Teddy?" I asked disastrously.

Curiously, it was skinny, ugly Miss Peabody who flashed into my mind at that point. Of all the teachers I ever had, I like her best. She never says anything but the truth, and she never pretends that things that hurt don't hurt. "Don't ever ask anyone to like you, Melissa. It's the surest way to earn their contempt." I don't know what the occasion was or why she said it. But the words had stayed with me, and they blared now in a sharp warning signal that came too late.

Teddy stuck his hands in his back pockets. "Well, sure. I mean, in a way. Maybe you should go into women's lib, though, come to think of it. Somewhere where you don't have to be attractive to the male. Physically, that is."

It was as though winter moved into my heart. It was useless to tell myself that he was stupid, the way Father said. (After all, Father didn't think much of me as a female, either.) Or that Teddy was insensitive. If he were sensitive he would think it and not say it. Would that make it any better?

Yes. But not much.

There's a saying: Today's the first day of the rest of your life. I heard the words as Teddy shifted his feet in embarrassment. Something on my face must have gotten through even to him. "Look," he mumbled, "you shouldn'a asked me. I didn't mean . . . that is, Claire said . . ."

Claire. Of course.

Claire, with her waist-length straight fair hair and light, supple body, whom my father described as a hip blend of Alice in Wonderland and Aphrodite. It was Claire Father followed with his eyes at school plays and shows, whenever he did turn up. I know. I watched him. Even Mother was hooked on Claire as the perfect adolescent female.

17

Not above playing off my parents one against the other, I once said to Mother, "Father thinks she's just about God's version of the ideal daughter."

"Yes," Mother snapped. "He would."

Hope surged into my heart. "You don't think she's attractive?"

Mother looked at me. "Of course she's attractive. It's a thousand pities you don't use her as a model. . . ." I didn't hear the rest. It wasn't important.

Is it any wonder that I hated Claire with total passion? And now Teddy. I took a step backward.

"Good-bye, Teddy," I said. "It hasn't been particularly nice knowing you."

"What d'ya mean, good-bye? You movin' or something?"

"Only out of your life."

"Never thought you were in it, except, of course, living next door."

"Thanks. It's lovely to be appreciated. Next time you want somebody to do your English composition, ask Claire. With her grasp of spelling and grammar you both ought to make remedial class in a week. You can sit in the back and cuddle."

One of the troubles is I'm only five two. Teddy stood looking down at me. I learned then that you can never depend one hundred percent on anything. Not even Teddy's stupidity.

"You're jealous."

"Of what?" I put all the sarcasm I could into it. "Claire's brains?"

"Brains aren't everything."

I reminded myself that it was one of the dumber re-
marks of all time. I had to, because I could feel the hot,
swollen sensation at the back of my throat and eyes that
meant I wanted to cry. When I suddenly remembered that
Miss Peabody had also said it I could almost feel the tears
spring forward. To stall them I said, "You just stick to that,
Teddy, and you won't suffer a minute's self-doubt."

I walked away up the long slope of our lawn to the
front door and into the house. Then I stood in the hall, waiting, although I didn't know what for. After a minute or two
I realized I was wondering if I should go into Father's study
and ask him if he thought I was attractive as a female—
which just shows how shook I was, even to think of such a
thing. I was still standing there when the study door opened
and he came out. He glanced at me. "What's the matter,
Melissa?"

Words vanished from me. I gave a long, shuddering
sigh and started to cry.

"What in God's name—Melissa, what's the matter?"

It might have been the beginning of something. But at
that minute Mother came running out of the living room.
"What happened? Richard! What did you say to her?"

"Nothing. I came out of the room, saw she was upset,
asked her what the matter was, and she burst into tears. I
haven't said anything."

"Well, it would be just like you. You're always saying
vicious, cutting things that wound. I wouldn't put it past
you to have deliberately bullied her."

My father walked past me to the front door. With his
hand on the doorknob he turned and said, "I have always
thought the ancient and mediaeval custom of keeping

women in secluded parts of houses where their outbursts of hysteria would not interfere with the rational course of life a very sensible idea." With that he opened the door.

Mother said, "That left you men alone to enjoy yourselves and have everything your own way, didn't it? I've always said—"

Partly to drown it all out I wailed harder than ever. My father looked towards me.

"Aren't you too old for that? Don't you have any dignity?" His quiet voice sliced through me.

I pulled my hands away from my face and looked at him. I knew I had been making an unholy racket. Part of me was taking pleasure in it. I don't know what I thought it would do for me. Get his attention? Well, I had got it. His finely etched face radiated distaste. "You're two of a kind."

"Thanks a lot," Mother said indignantly. Her hands nervously pulled at her sweater and smoothed it over her stomach.

I took a breath and wiped the tears off my cheeks. "It's not a compliment, Mother," I said unnecessarily.

"Melissa—" Father started. And then, "Oh, forget it!" And he walked out the door, closing it after him.

Two

At the time I didn't know that day was the big divide. I just knew that I was more miserable than I had ever been before.

Father didn't get home until late that night. Where he was neither Mother nor I knew, although both of us guessed. I knew she didn't know, because if she had known, she would have casually dropped the information. But she sat through dinner never mentioning him. Halfway through dinner she asked me what I had been crying about. Until that moment I think she had forgotten. What Father had said had pushed it out of the way.

Remembering still hurt, and I didn't know which hurt more, what Teddy said or what Father said later. But from somewhere a new steeliness had come into me. It was as though I hurt so much that it didn't matter anymore.

"Teddy said I would never be attractive to the male and should join women's lib."

Mother took the bait as I knew she would. In less than a minute she was off and running on the subject of women's lib and how being rejected by the male had nothing to do with it. Nothing. "Not, of course," Mother said, veering abruptly, "that Teddy isn't right about you in one way. Melissa, you *have* to go on a diet. You'll never attract boys looking like that. I've told you and told you, and the time is long overdue that—"

I don't know what got into me. I stood up and screamed. "Leave me alone. I won't go on a diet. I don't care if I'm fat. I hate men. I don't care if I never see another one. I hate you and I hate Father. LEAVE ME ALONE. Or I'll leave home. I mean it, Mother. I'll leave."

Funny. Until that second I hadn't realized that I did mean it. But all of a sudden, as though it were a movie in front of me, I could see myself in jeans and poncho in some commune miles and miles away on the other side of the country with a lot of people who didn't give the time of day what I looked like. There, in my commune, nobody cared what anybody looked like. It was as real as Mother sitting there, and I wanted it more than I had ever wanted anything, even Teddy, I decided.

Mother just sat there, her mouth open. We stared at each other. Then, as though pulled, my eyes went to the side where there was an oval gold mirror reflecting both of us. Suddenly I wanted to laugh, because if anyone had been asked to pick out the about-to-be high school dropout, they would have pointed to Mother. With her waif face, Mia Farrow haircut and huge blue eyes, turtleneck sweater clanking with rows and rows of silver chain and love beads, she looked younger than I did and like the commune personified. And me? Brown straight hair, brown eyes, round chubby face, round chubby chest, also a turtleneck which didn't make me look like a youthful seaman, it made me look like a bullfrog. I stared at my image, loathing it. Then I said to Mother, "You look like the hippie. You've got a thing about youth being the big deal. Why don't you go out with Teddy and try and beat Claire's time?"

"Melissa darling—"

"Don't talk to me, Mother. I don't want to talk." I stormed into the hall, looked for my jacket which wasn't in the hall closet and went out, slamming the front door behind me.

The mystics all have their mountaintop or wilderness. I have the town library, open till ten o'clock every night.

I don't know why I like our local library so much. Probably because it's about to be torn down. They're building a new one out nearer the high school with modern stacks, air conditioning and all the latest improvements. The old one is straight out of a Victorian horror novel—all ceiling, huge areas of totally wasted space, poor heating, no air conditioning, a filing system that causes librarians to leave in droves for other suburbs, and a pervasive smell of books and bad breath. The bad breath is, I think, donated by a couple of town drunks and derelicts who use the library to snooze in. There was one ancient and highly aromatic character who always took out Gibbon's *Decline and Fall of the Roman Empire*, over which to do his snoozing, which I thought showed very good taste. Periodically a reform group sweeps out the drunks, buys air spray and gives free lectures on the importance of books. There's a benefit of some kind. A sum of money is collected, the derelicts disappear and the grumbling dies down. Then, a week or so later, the vagrants come shivering back and everything settles down to normal. I rather like them.

But I hadn't been to the library in some time. In my manic periods I have always charted and plotted campaigns for getting thin and getting Teddy. When I start feeling depressed I go back to eating and to the library. I decided to stop being a manic-depressive and start being a schizophrenic. It gave me more scope. Reality, I decided, was for the birds.

There's probably something else I should mention about the library. It's where our local peddlers and pushers hang out. Since most of them take great trouble to look like Eagle Scouts, I think all the adults assume they're studying for their college boards. How can they be so stupid? But then adults are stupid most of the time, stupid and cruel and hypocritical. Or so I felt tonight.

I went straight to the stacks, which is something in the old library that is hard to prevent, and is probably why the librarians are so eager to move into new quarters. Anyway, all I had to do was slip to the right as I came in, circle around the magazine stands and racks and there I was.

But the stacks weren't any good tonight, either. The moment I got there a smattering of titters and scuffles hit my ear and that was the last thing I wanted to hear. I snatched the nearest book off the nearest shelf and walked out into the reading room.

I sat there at one of the tables. There was a reading lamp above each section of the table, but I didn't turn mine on. In the dusky light I stared at the title of the book I pulled out. It was an anatomy book. What it was doing on that shelf I don't know. The medical section was over on the other side. Anyway, there it was. I opened the book at random. A lot of other people must have been opening the book at random because it fell open to a page as though there had been a marker. The huge illustration, covering the entire page, stared up at me: the human body, male gender. The original artist had been meticulous, scientific and detached. What had been added in red crayon was neither scientific nor meticulous: passionate, more like, and graphic. I stared at the soaring, swollen monstrosity, fascinated and sickened. Mother had been trying to tell me about the facts of life—about sex and all that—for years, but I had always managed to stop her. For some reason, I had felt it was a collection of facts I could live without. Now I wished I had let her. I might have got used to the idea. What I could not seem to keep out of my head was a series of home movies going on in my mind featuring Father and his girl friend. I shut the book and sat there, propping my face up, elbows on the table.

When I felt a hand on my shoulder, I nearly jumped out of my skin.

"Sorry. I didn't mean to scare you," a familiar voice said gruffly.

I turned and looked up at Miss Peabody's beaky face.

"Are you all right?" she asked in her raspy whisper.

I realized then I was crying. The cover of the book was wet. I saw also that several people were watching me, including my friend the drunk, who seemed to keep his wavering, bleary gaze in my direction.

"Let's go," Miss Peabody said. She had on her tattered phantom-of-the-opera-type cloak and was clutching a couple of books under her arm.

"Okay," I muttered, embarrassed, and followed her towards the main door.

As I passed I saw Claire and Teddy huddled together, apparently reading out of one book at the end of one of the tables. Obviously Ted was going through one of his periodic phases of trying to push up his grades and get his mother off his back. (Mrs. MacDonald still cherished illusions about Ted's scholarly potential.) But I didn't know how much education he could be absorbing while he whispered in Claire's ear and his tan fingers played in and out of her yellow hair. They must have come in after I did, otherwise I certainly would have noticed them. I was noticing them hard as I went out, because I all but fell over an empty chair which slid screeching across the floor.

Everybody looked up, including Claire and Teddy. Claire giggled and whispered something to Ted. Ted snorted and then muffled his mouth behind his hand.

Suddenly, from the middle of the room the librarian, Mrs. Summers, spoke up. "Ted MacDonald and Claire Reynolds, if you're here to study, do so. If not, please go somewhere else."

Ted, thinking himself safe behind a stack of books, put his thumb to his nose. There were more giggles from those who could see. Among them was Miss Peabody whom he had forgotten and who didn't giggle.

"Ah yes, Ted," she said loudly. "A gesture known and used internationally. But I don't think Mrs. Summers had a chance to appreciate it. Stand up, now, and do it again."

It was one of those things that could have gone either way. Given his good looks and popularity, Ted could have done it with panache and made the librarian and the teacher look silly.

But Mrs. Summers was liked and respected and Miss Peabody had her own standing as a kind of brilliant kook.

"Yes, do, Ted. I'm sorry I missed it." Mrs. Summers sat back, a look of amusement on her elegant, wise face under the gray hair. "Don't keep us waiting."

My misery lightened considerably as Ted, brick red, rose to his feet, did a hasty retake of the gesture and sat down again.

"Thank you. Now we can all go back to work again. That is, if you will allow us."

Yummy, I thought, or at least part of me thought. Before Claire it would have been I who bound up his ego and loved doing it. I could almost replay the scene. As we walked home, or maybe the next day fooling around the yard or school grounds, Ted would go through the whole thing, stroke by stroke, only by the time he was finished certain subtle changes would have taken place: he hadn't been poking fun at me, his gesture had been a harmless, deliberately misunderstood joke, and Miss Peabody and Mrs. Summers were always in collusion to get him (why, of course, he would not have made entirely clear). I, his disciple and camp follower, would agree with all this, make soothing, reassuring noises, and as a reward would be allowed to stand outside his door listening to him for an hour before the royal interview was over and I was allowed to go home (unescorted).

The awful part was that I knew that if Ted, this minute, offered me the role again, I'd snatch at it.

It was a lowering thought. Even more lowering was the sheer unlikelihood of any such thing happening. As I followed Miss Peabody out I caught sight of myself in the glass of one of the library display cabinets and my gloom deepened. I looked like what Mother calls a Bovolopus (pronounced Bo-*vol*-opus). Where she got the word I don't know, but it's a recent acquisition. When Father asked her at dinner what a Bovolopus was, she said vaguely, "the kind of woman who wears hair curlers to the supermarket and takes up at least one and a half seats on any form of public transportation."

"When were you ever on some form of public transportation?" Father asked.

Mother bristled. "I was on a town bus last week, I'll have you know."

"Ah, yes. I remember. Your fender was being repaired. How did you enjoy your unexpected contact with the working classes?"

"You talk as though *I* were a snob. It's *you* who are."

"No, no. You're confused. I'm not a snob, I'm a reactionary."

"What's the diff— Oh, never mind! Melissa! I saw you. Put that potato back."

It's like all roads leading to Rome: all my parents' bickerings seem to lead to me and what I'm eating, probably because we're usually at dinner, since it's the one time we get together.

Now I looked quickly away from my image in the display cabinet and slipped out the door behind Miss Peabody. When we got to the bottom of the library steps Miss Peabody stopped. She looked at me.

"Home?"

I didn't want to go home. It was only eight thirty. If Father were there it would be bad. If he weren't it would be worse, because then Mother would be alone and fidgety, and if I turned up she would take out her fidgetiness by embarking on her favorite project: me. Her constant, never-ending campaign for the improvement and making over of Melissa never pauses, rests or stops.

"No. I think I'll go—" I was about to say "to the coffee shop" but I changed it to "for a walk." Miss Peabody had never yet commented on my eating habits, but I wasn't handing her any cue.

She stood there, looking ungainly as always, and switched her books from one arm to another, dropping one of the books in transit. I picked it up.

"Oh, thank you, Melissa. Clumsy of me." She said it absently. I wondered suddenly if she minded being clumsy and awkward and I tried to imagine what she might have looked like when she was my age. The trouble was, I couldn't. She settled her books. "Like to go for a drive?"

I was surprised. In all the years I'd been taught by her both in elementary and then high school I'd never seen Miss Peabody in any other than a school situation. "Yes. I'd like to. Thanks."

Miss Peabody's car always reminded me of an angry red beetle. It's a small foreign type that makes a fearful clatter and is sometimes seen taking corners on two wheels, not so much because of speed, but because (it is said) Miss Peabody likes to turn corners that way and has trained Ferdinand accordingly. Ferdinand, her car, is almost as well known as she is.

"How's Ferdinand?" I asked, as we crossed the street to a small parking lot reserved for the library.

"He's not been himself lately. Awfully quiet. He hasn't snorted once since I brought him back from the repair place."

"Maybe it's because he was repaired."

"Of course. That was what I took him there for. But he'll soon be himself again."

"You sound as though you like him to make noise, Miss Peabody. What about noise pollution?"

"If you're going to go ecological on me I'll drop you at your house. It may surprise you to know that I find his mechanical sounds very soothing after a day in school surrounded by purely human noises."

It didn't surprise me at all.

Miss Peabody backed into the driver's seat and I squeezed in on the other side. After Ferdinand's coughing, spitting and revving had been properly listened to, Miss Peabody nosed him out into the street, pushed him in gear and roared past the library. We drove through some of the poorer sections, out across the Post Road and up into the open country lying beyond the town.

It was just dark; there was half a moon and a smell of hay and grass through the window. Miss Peabody and I talked about school, which had just started, the drama club for which she was consultant, and the play which she wanted us to do.

"Why *Antigone*?" I asked.

"It's a good play. Have you read it?"

"No. And I know some of the other kids in the club have other ideas about what we ought to do. Something more modern. More relevant."

Miss Peabody moaned. "Relevant! It used to be such a nice word. It had impact. Now it's just a cliché."

"Well, you know what I mean, Miss Peabody."

"I do. And I think you'll find *Antigone* very relevant."

"What's it about?"

"Well, it's about principle versus political compromise. Can you think of anything more relevant?"

I grinned in the dark.

"Read it, Melissa, and see for yourself."

"All right."

We drove for a while in silence, which is something that can be very pleasant. No demands, no wondering what the other person is thinking and how soon they're going to pounce or what improvement they're about to point out you can make on yourself.

As we turned back into the town and neared my street Miss Peabody suddenly said, "Ted MacDonald will probably be a reasonable and pleasant human being in about a dozen years' time if—but only if—he's lucky enough to have a few ego-deflating experiences between now and then. But until that happens he will remain the good-looking insensitive block we all know and endure."

We drew up in front of my house. She leaned on her

steering wheel and gently revved Ferdinand a few times. "And if you quote me on any of that, Melissa, I'll deny it all." She turned. "When you next feel like you're going into a depression over what King Ted, or anyone, thinks of you, why don't you turn it around and see what you think —*think,* not just feel—about him or her or it or them? It has a very exhilarating effect. More heads have been taken out of more ovens doing that. Gently with Ferdinand's door. Don't slam it. Read *Antigone.* I want you to have a part in the play. No—don't argue. Good night."

And off she roared down the street.

Mother was engrossed in a TV movie. There was no sign of Father, so I crept up to bed. Right before I went to sleep I found myself again wondering what Miss Peabody was like when she was my age. Oddly, this time I could, dimly, imagine it: younger, of course, but still all elbows and nose and big pigeon-toed feet. No wonder her words were like a hand under my heart. She knew.

Three

The next morning I awoke feeling a little better, which lasted until I went to the closet for my jumper and caught my reflection in the full-length mirror set into the outside of the closet door.

"It will encourage you with your dieting," Mother had said when she had Joseph, the neighborhood handyman, remove the mirror from the inside of the door and put it on the outside. She had engineered this sneakily while I was at school so when I got home I was confronted with a *fait accompli*—and myself. It didn't encourage me with my dieting; I had merely perfected the art of approaching the closet door without having to look at it—very useful in the general technique of ambushing an enemy without his knowing you're there, but not helpful in what Miss Peabody would call the daily grind, the common task.

In my overall euphoria I had forgotten all about it, so there I was staring at myself, glorious in navy blue bra, psychedelic slip and extra poundage. I sucked in my cheeks and stomach and smoothed my bangs. Then I stuck my tongue out, crossed my eyes and flung open the door. After I had yanked my jumper and sweater out, I left the closet door open, which always riles Mother. "Why do you think I went to the trouble of putting the mirror there?" she asks, if I happen to be there while she's closing it. Then she stands in front of it, fluffing her hair and smoothing whatever's in front of her flat stomach. You can see why there's a failure of communication between us.

I went downstairs to breakfast and found Father, who I thought had stayed in town for the night, sitting there, buried in the editorial section of the *Times*. If there's anything drearier than breakfast with Mother and me, it's breakfast with all of us. Father doesn't like early morning chatter. So Mother, who does, exudes a sense of repression. When I grow up I intend to have breakfast alone with my dog. We don't have a dog because Mother wants a poodle and Father wants what he calls a dog dog, not (and I quote) "some decorator's beribboned monstrosity," so we don't have any dog at all. Fortunately or unfortunately (since I haven't yet decided whether I am going to be a poet turning out a few incomparable gemlike lines when not battling the harsh realities of a materialistic society, or a biologist pouring my life's strength into the wretched masses struggling to be free), my mind is inclined to slide into rather corny rhymes.

The family that prays together, stays together, I thought, pouring myself some cereal. And then, without, as they say, a pause, came the next line: *The family that stays together slays together.* How apt. I gave a sort of giggle that I tried to turn into a cough.

"Something amusing you?" Father asked.

I looked at him quickly, to see if he was being sarcastic, wondering what he was doing last night and who he was doing it with. "No."

Mother emerged from her paper. "Did you catch cold? You left without your jacket."

"How could she catch cold? It may have been damp, but it couldn't have been below sixty degrees."

"I didn't think you had time to notice," Mother said, staring at him over Eugenia Sheppard's column in *Women's Wear Daily* which she reads daily to find out, Father once said, what she is going to think for the rest of the day.

They were off and running. I slurped down the last of my milk and cornflakes and got up from the table. " 'Bye."

To my horror Father got up, too. "Wait, Melissa, I'll drive you."

One of the things I had been carefully keeping out of my mind was what Father had said last night during the general brouhaha. It wasn't something a body cares to think about. And one of the best ways of keeping it out of my mind was to stay as far from Father as possible.

"You'll miss your train," I said, edging towards the door.

Father picked up his briefcase and raincoat. "Then I'll catch the next."

"There's no reason for that. I know you like to get to the office early. Besides, I like to walk."

"I'll take you," he said. And that was that.

"Brace yourself," Mother commented, going back to Eugenia.

Father stopped in the doorway. "Thank you. Was that necessary? Do you really feel that my daughter and I can't go a few yards in the car without cosmic disaster?"

"Ask her."

Father opened his mouth. I decided the moment to split had come. "Don't let me keep you from your quarrel," I muttered and launched myself doorwards. But not very far. Father's hand had circled my arm.

I guess he must have decided that this particular skirmish in our family's hundred years' war could be postponed. Looking like a newspaper picture of the FBI in a successful capture we marched out the front door and along the path leading to the garage and the car.

"In you go," Father said. Then he went round the side and got behind the steering wheel. While he was easing the car down the driveway and I was sitting there wondering if I could take the Fifth, Teddy ambled out of the house next door.

I decided to forget (temporarily) that he had broken my heart. My need was greater than my pride. "How about giving Teddy a lift?" I said and started frantically rolling down the window.

"No," Father said, shoved the car in gear and shot into the street.

We drove in silence for a while. I was beginning to let myself hope that he really did mean just to give me a ride when he cleared his throat and said, "I'm sorry for some of the things I said yesterday, Melissa."

"Then why did you say them?"

He hesitated. "Don't you ever say things you don't mean?"

I thought about the things I had yelled at Mother.

"Yes. At least, not exactly. I may be sorry I said them, but that doesn't mean I don't mean them."

I waited to see how he'd handle that. Would he say he didn't mean what he'd said? If he did I wouldn't believe him. And if he didn't say so—and convince me he meant it —I'd hate him. Heads you win, tails I lose. But did that apply to him or to me? Without thinking I said the words aloud.

Father drew the car up a block or so, behind the school. "What do you mean by that?"

"You'll miss your train."

"As I said before, then I'll catch the next. What do you mean by 'Heads you win, tails I lose'?"

I really wanted to get out of that car. "There's Miss Peabody," I said as her cloak flapped into sight around the corner.

He reached out and took hold of my chin, pulling my face around. "What did you mean, Melissa?"

It's curious. I can almost never remember Father touching me when I was smaller. He's not a person who goes around casually touching people, not even Mother. And now, when he does touch me, I get embarrassed and uncomfortable. I blurted out, "Because I think you meant what you said last night, about my not having any dignity and Mother and me being two of a kind. You weren't exactly saying how much you like us. In fact, you sounded as though you found us repulsive."

Father dropped his hand back to the steering wheel. I looked at it there: strong, shapely, long-fingered. I looked at my own lying on my jumper skirt, short-fingered and stubby.

"I'm sorry. I didn't mean that you—Well, if I did sound annoyed, it was because you were howling as though you were a ten-year-old, not like a girl who two and a half years from now will be legally an adult, able to marry and vote."

Anger surged up in me. "I know you don't really like Mother very much—in fact, you're always making fun of her. And she turns me off a lot, too, always trying to make me be something else. But at least, after dinner, she *asked* me what I was crying about."

Father flushed. His voice developed that knife edge that always undoes me. "What do you mean saying I don't like your mother? And anyway, I did ask you as soon as I came out of my study and saw you there."

"You didn't want to know what was bothering me. You wanted to know why I was making all that noise."

"Melissa, I will not be talked to like that, not by anyone. Certainly not by my fifteen-year-old daughter."

"It's just like I said, Daddy. Heads you win, tails I lose. One minute I'm almost an adult and shouldn't behave like a child. The next minute, when I try and talk to you as though I *were* an adult, all of a sudden I'm a child and mustn't be rude to my elders. You have it both ways."

Running out of courage, I pushed open the door and got out quickly. " 'Bye, Daddy," I yelled and slammed the door.

I saw him staring at me for a moment, then he turned and drove off.

I wasn't feeling sociable, but since Miss Peabody was only about ten feet away I had to wait for her.

"Wasn't that your father, Melissa?"

"Yes."

"You looked as though you could hardly wait to get rid of him."

As usual, she was on target. But it made me furious. "You have no right to say that."

"Why not? I didn't say it was that way. I just said it looked that way. As for rights, don't you believe in free speech?"

"You shouldn't judge on looks," I said piously.

"Just what I've always said. But nobody believes me. By now I'd be married and have ten children if people thought that."

"Do you want to be married and have ten children?"

"Guess not, or I would have arranged it." And she gave that loud cackle that passes for a laugh.

Well, if she believed that, fine. But who would ever have wanted to marry her? My irritation receded before a warm, faintly smug tide of compassion. Poor thing.

But her ESP, always good, was working. "Somebody did propose to me once."

"Why did he change his mind?" I asked, and then realized the appalling implications of my question.

"It would seem to be that way, wouldn't it? But, in fact, I did."

"I'm sorry . . . I didn't mean . . . Why did you turn him down?"

We had stopped and she was moving her books from one arm to the other in that irritating way she has. Of course one dropped. I stooped and picked it up. "You ought to get one of those strap things and tie your books together, Miss Peabody."

"Then I'd drop the whole caboodle and it would be much heavier for you to pick up. In answer to your question, it seemed like a good thing to do at the time."

Not being retarded, I got the point of what she was saying: it's not just the Miss Americas that say no.

All right. But what kind of a guy was he? All glasses and buck teeth? And probably B.O.? Or just somebody like—a picture leaped to my mind—the school oddball, Joel Martin.

"Later on he got the Nobel Prize," Miss Peabody said, still tracking my thoughts.

That sounded like something Joel could do, too. He was either in the science lab or in a book. Never into people.

"Oh. What for?"

"Something in physics. Listen, Melissa, you're going to come to the play reading this afternoon, aren't you?"

"I don't want a part, Miss Peabody."

"Why? Just because Ted and Claire will probably be in it? What are you going to do—slink off every time they come near? Stop doing everything they do, including maybe breathing or living?"

We'd really got down to the nitty gritty. "I'm too fat to be on a stage," I said baldly.

Miss Peabody tugged at her cloak and I waited for some asinine adult remark such as "People are always wanting to take it off, put it on or rearrange it. Ha-ha."

"There are parts other than the lead. There are different kinds of costumes. And you don't know what effect being in a play might have on you. I mean—don't lock yourself into a do-nothing pattern. That's just putting more bars on the cage. Get a part. Who knows what might happen then?"

"You mean it might all fall off?"

"Don't you ever think about anything else? The way you look at things might change. Or something you can't imagine now might happen." She stared down at me, while I mentally rejected almost all of what she said.

"Look at the converse, Melissa. If you don't take a part, if you don't do the things you want to do, is this going to make you automatically stop eating or provide some magic? Or are you going to eat more out of sheer boredom and frustration? Think about it. I've got to go now. See you this afternoon. Oh, sorry!"

I picked up her book again and handed it to her and she took off.

Four

Later that afternoon I turned up in the auditorium for the discussion of the selection and casting of the school Christmas play. All the kids interested in the school theater were there, and if sound waves could do it, the roof should have been floating away. Everybody was screaming. Eventually I sorted it out to three unequal factions, the smallest consisting of a few diehard traditionalists who were plugging *The Taming of the Shrew*. Another bunch wanted *A Streetcar Named Desire* and the ones making most of the noise wanted *Who's Afraid of Virginia Woolf?*

"The last two require first-class acting, of which we haven't enough," Miss Peabody said. She was standing three feet away, near the piano on which were stacked ten identical books.

"Be quiet! All of you!" The clear, strong voice of the drama coach, Miss Ainslie, carried above the din.

There was silence almost immediately.

"All right. I understand most of you don't want to do Shakespeare even though it's always been the custom for the Christmas play, but in case you care, there are going to be two other productions of *Streetcar* in Westchester this Christmas."

The *Streetcar* faction quieted to a mumble, while the *Virginia Woolf* crew started yelling louder than ever.

"How many of you have actually seen *Virginia Woolf* performed?"

Seven hands went up.

"Where?"

The answers came to one road show, three summer stock productions and the movie.

"All right. How were the productions?"

One of the girls, a senior named Nancy Feldman, giggled. "The one I saw was awful. The audience laughed in all the wrong places." There was reluctant agreement among the others who had seen stock productions.

"Precisely. A play like *Virginia Woolf* takes top acting or it's a farce—literally. Now who'd like to be on stage when that happens?"

Miss Ainslie, who had been both on the Broadway stage and in English repertory, had made her point. Nobody wanted to be on stage holding the ball while the audience tittered.

43

"Clever," Miss Peabody said. She had moved to one of the seats near me.

"Why?"

"Use your head. Can't you imagine how some of the parents would react to Albee's language, particularly those from Woodville East? Especially when you remember who our star actress is."

"Oh."

Woodville East was our local hard-hat contingency, consisting, as Mother once put it, of dozens and dozens of Archie Bunkers. According to Mother, who was last year's PTA president, they could be depended upon to vote down every progressive step the school board and the PTA introduced. And as for sex education in schools, Mother swore one night at home after a turbulent meeting that they sat in a bunch and did nothing but say no to any course more inflammatory than a lecture on cross-pollination.

"They're against sex," she stormed, making herself a third drink. "There they live, exploding the population at every opportunity with about twelve children per family, and they won't even discuss it."

"They can't be against sex, then," Father said. "They're just against talking about it. I'm on their side."

"You would be."

Anyway, I saw now what Miss Peabody meant. Especially since the star actress of the drama club was their own Ann O'Faolin. The O'Faolins, father and daughter (mother had long since run off with somebody), lived in the heart of Bunkerdom, and, according to local gossip, O'Faolin père could be seen four nights out of five being poured out of

Tim's Tavern where he staunchly and regularly fought the good fight against communism, socialism, liberalism, radicalism, kids, long hair, the twentieth century, *The New York Times* and sex education in schools.

Ann O'Faolin is a quiet, medium-sized, average-looking girl with slightly large features, until she gets up on stage. At that point some kind of magic happens and she stops being medium or average anything. She blazes like a light, and if she's on the stage it's an effort to look at anyone else. It isn't that she upstages anyone or uses what Miss Ainslie calls clever bits of business to attract attention. She doesn't have to do *anything* except just be there. Miss Ainslie says it's called stage presence. Whatever it is, Ann has it, squared, cubed and in depth. As a matter of course, she's the female lead in any production the school puts on, and for once nobody argues except, of course, Mrs. Reynolds, Claire's mother, who feels that any plum going around should be Claire's.

Anyway, in the silence that followed the routing of the *Virginia Woolf* forces, Miss Ainslie said, "Miss Peabody and I have another suggestion. How about Sophocles' *Antigone*? It's one of the great Greek classical plays, which should keep the straights quiet, but inside its traditional form a lot of contemporary points are made and any women's libber among you should be overjoyed."

There was an immediate babble. "We just happen to have a few copies here," Miss Ainslie said in casual spoof, reaching up to the books on the piano. Amid the ensuing giggles she passed them around. "Look." She checked her watch. "We've got the rest of the afternoon. How about a trial reading? Tryouts will be later this afternoon, but I'd like to begin with a sample reading of the first act now to give you a feel of the play."

Miss Peabody hissed, "Go on up front, Melissa. I want you in it. At least you can be in the chorus. Go *on*," she repeated, as I hung back. Then she leaned forward and gave me a shove and I went on up to the front near the stage and stood beside Ann O'Faolin. Ann and Sally Mayhew are about my best friends at school, although I guess Sally and I are closer. At least we chatter and giggle together a lot more. It isn't that I don't like Ann as much, it's just that she's more aloof.

"Now," Miss Ainslie said. "There are only five real parts, so most of the rest of you are going to be in the chorus. And before anybody walks out in a huff, let me tell you that the chorus in a Greek play is as important as any single character, with as much training and discipline, if not more, than a single role. You're going to be drilled as though you were the Rockettes. Why don't any of you who would like to be in the chorus go and stand over here."

Miss Ainslie waved her right arm as most of us shuffled over to where she stood. "No, don't clutter around me in front. I want you on my right."

I found myself near Sally, who had come in late.

"You don't want to be in the chorus, do you?" I said to her, knowing her secret stage ambitions. "Don't you want a part?"

"I'm not good enough," Sally whispered. For some reason she was very shy and embarrassed about being stage-struck. I think she was afraid of being laughed at.

"You won't know till you try," I said unoriginally.

"Well, what about you? Why don't you try for a part?"

I almost said, "I'm not that stuck on it." But a sudden impulse of honesty made me say what I had said to Miss Peabody. "I'm too fat."

"Quiet, you two," Miss Ainslie said. She, Ann O'Faolin and Miss Peabody were in a huddle. Off to one side, leaning his splendid muscles against the wall, was Ted Mac-Donald. Leaning possessively against Ted's muscles was Claire. My heart gave an unhappy squeeze. I forced myself back to Sally who had been whispering. "What did you say?" I asked.

"I don't know why you don't at least try."

"Try what?"

"What I told you. You weren't listening. A diet pill."

"They're supposed to be bad for you."

"Not if you use them properly and not take more than you're supposed to. Anyway, that's what my aunt did. She said she only took it for about two or three weeks and after that it was a breeze and she didn't have to take any pills any more."

"Did she lose?"

"Pounds! Tons!"

Miss Ainslie turned towards us again and we both shut up.

"Now," she said, "I've asked Ann to read Antigone. Go up on the stage, Ann." She turned around. "Ted Mac-Donald? Are you here?" My heart gave another squeeze as Miss Ainslie looked over the hall. "There you are. Come on up front. Why don't you, for now, read Haemon, Antigone's betrothed?"

The way Ted walked up the auditorium and onto the stage it was as though a band were playing "Hail to the Chief."

Miss Ainslie's eyes traveled over the room. "Now who'll read for Creon, both king and villain?"

There were several noisy suggestions which she ignored. "As I told you, these are readings. Anyone who wants to try out may do so later."

And then she gave us a real shock. "Joel Martin. Come up here. I want you to read Creon."

This time there was general mutter. "Joel, for Pete's sake!" somebody behind me said not too softly.

"Yes. Joel. I have a suspicion he will do it very well."

I didn't even think he'd be here since he practically never joins in school activities. But he was, sitting at the back, by himself, as usual.

"Joel!"

For a minute he didn't move, then he got up and walked slowly down the center aisle. As he passed he took the book Miss Ainslie was holding out and went up onto the stage.

Joel is odd-looking, medium height and thin, with ears that stick out a little and very thick glasses. Also, there is something slightly funny about his upper lip. I think it's because there's a scar running straight down into it from the bottom of his nose. He doesn't very often say anything, and when he does, half the time it's sarcastic. He isn't from around here, but came to live with his father about two years ago. Where his mother is, if he has any, I don't know. Nor where he lived before.

Up on the stage Ann, Joel and Ted seemed to be

reading their texts; that is, Joel was reading his, and Ann and Ted seemed to be discussing hers. Then Claire Reynolds caught my eye, and I saw instantly that the really interesting show was not on the stage. Claire's great violet eyes took in Teddy and Ann reading out of the same book and turned a murderous glare towards Miss Ainslie. Claire's sentiments could be read at forty yards. If Ted was going to play some kind of Romeo to Antigone, then nobody, but nobody, should play Antigone except Claire Reynolds. I could all but read the note her mother would certainly be writing to the principal. The whole thing almost made up for my general low spirits.

"Claire's furious," I whispered ecstatically to Sally.

Sally grinned. "For once the Fair Claire will lose. Miss Ainslie can match muscle power with her any time. And she's a million light-years ahead of her in brains." (Sally, the theater buff, is one of Miss Ainslie's more ardent admirers.) "But it's a pity she has to waste time picking off that boring member of the rich elite. If the principal weren't such a gutless—" Sally, who is also very politically oriented, was just getting into her best radical rhetoric when Miss Ainslie suddenly turned around and said, for the third time, "Quiet! Can't you two stop talking for five seconds? Maybe what you need is something to keep you occupied. Sally, come on up here. I want you to read the part of Ismene, Antigone's sister, the second female role."

Sally went from brick red to white, except for her freckles, which stood out like confetti. "I'm not—" she started, her voice croaking.

"Yes, you are and you can. This is only a reading. Come along now. There's a good child. Don't argue."

49

There was warmth and kindness, as well as sheer bossiness in Miss Ainslie's voice. Sally handed me her books, took a text and went up on the stage. Beside Ann, who's average height and size, Sally looked tiny.

"Now, let's see. Who'll read Queen Eurydice?" Her eyes slid around the room.

Bereft of Sally, I reverted to habit and turned my gaze towards Teddy. He was standing between Ann and Sally in a kind of graceful slouch. The center light poured down on his thick, waving reddish hair. Beside him, Joel looked like a total zero. Mr. Foureyes Blah, as some of the kids called him. Nevertheless, he managed to create the impression he was on an uninhabited island entirely by his own choice. If anybody was a true loner, it was Joel Martin, and with the light reflected off his spectacles and totally hiding his eyes he looked like a space goblin or UFO.

"Melissa!"

I had been so busy watching the leads on stage that it came as something of a shock to find Miss Ainslie was watching me. I stared back at her.

"Melissa, I'd like to haul you out of the chorus to do Eurydice. Your voice is right for it, and I have an idea you could do it."

Part of me was wildly elated. The other part wanted none of it. Me, up there for people to laugh at? No, thanks. I could imagine what Father would say, how he would look. Even more easily could I imagine how Mother would react. It would be string beans and dried chicken till after the New Year. I opened my mouth to refuse, when Miss Ainslie went on.

"The trouble is, you don't exactly *look* like a tragic

Greek queen, haggard with suffering." I knew the laughs were good-natured, even as they seared my skin like hot bacon fat. I went into my role of class clown, roly-poly comic turn.

"Sorry about that," I chirruped with just the right impudence.

"How about a diet? You've got three months."

Deep inside my Bert Lahr role I was so angry and humiliated I felt sick. But if I showed one-millionth of it I would lose. What I would lose, I wasn't sure. But whatever it was, it was more important than anything else.

I was, in a sense, flying blind, feeling my part as I went alone. And then the heavens opened and handed me the script. And the *dea ex machina* was, of all people, Claire. She shook back her shining hair. "I don't think she can help it, Miss Ainslie. Some people can't. Compulsive overeating is a compensatory neurosis and quite, quite incurable."

To keep from crying I thought about how someday I would very slowly kill and dismember Claire.

There was a horrible silence. And then to everybody's astonishment, Joel flew down from his eyrie. "That's really interesting, Claire. Who wrote it out for you? How long did it take you to learn it?"

Claire, all of a sudden, looked frail, helpless and persecuted. Ted bunched his fists and stepped forward. "Of all—"

"That's enough!" Miss Ainslie stared at Claire. "How predictable," she said drily. She wheeled back to the stage where Ted had moved towards Joel. "And furthermore, Ted, if you start anything on stage now, you'll lose your chance for the part. It's up to you."

It was really delectable watching Ted struggle between Claire and his vanity. His vanity won. He shrugged and stayed where he was.

"Now, Melissa," Miss Ainslie said curtly, "get up on the stage and read Queen Eurydice."

"I'd rather be in the chorus, Miss Ainslie."

She directed one of her more ego-shriveling looks at me. "Nonsense. Now do as I say and give me a decent reading. You can, you know."

Yes, I was quite sure I could. I could feel it in my bones. But I was still hesitating when Joel spoke up again. "Come on, Mel. The queen isn't supposed to be a sex symbol—whatever that is—and we've wasted enough time futzing around." ·

I went up.

After that the reading went off pretty well. I could tell the way Sally read that she was trying to make me feel better. Ted, I was delighted to observe, sounded as wooden as he looked handsome. The real surprise was Joel. He was good. I'd never particularly noticed his voice before, maybe because he used it so little. But when he started to read, it didn't sound loud or strained. It was just tremendously clear, resonant, but not chesty or what I think of as purple. It was beautiful. It almost gave me goose bumps. Who'd have thought it of old Joel?

We came to the end and everybody, including me, liked the play. Between Sally and Joel, I forgot how I looked and got caught up in the action and really enjoyed my part. The other kids who were watching applauded with surprising enthusiasm, especially in the places where Antigone seemed to be making points for civil disobedience, Greek-style, B.C.

"All right, everybody," Miss Ainslie said. "That isn't bad at all. It should give the rest of you an idea of what I want when you do your readings. Everybody now on stage, off. Any others who want to read for one of the parts, over here."

In the end, after nearly two hours of readings, the parts remained where they were at first. Probably Miss Ainslie meant it that way from the beginning. But everyone who wanted a reading had had one, and the cast as originally set was accorded general approval. Obviously, Miss Ainslie had chosen the best people for that particular play, and anyway, as she reminded them, there'd be another play at Easter and another in June, all with different casts: everybody would have a chance.

"Okay," she said. "Everybody but the cast can go home. I want to see all backstage people, lighting assistants, costume designers and so on at three tomorrow."

"Now," she said, after they had left, "I want to talk to you about the play. I said it was about civil rights and tyranny. But it is also—mainly—about what the Greeks call hubris, which means pride or arrogance, and how the gods punish anyone who is guilty of it, as Creon is. He defies a law of the gods, a divine law, in favor of what he thinks is the good of the state, and in a fascinating, logical sequence of events, destroys everything he loves and values most. It's a play about law in cause and effect, about the clash of wills between Creon, the state, and Antigone, the rebel, who is yet obedient to divine law. It's about justice. It's one of the great plays of the world and it deserves everything you've got.

"Okay. That's all of that. Now from the great to the merely important. Since I've started with Melissa on helpful hints for self-improvement I'll continue the good work. I don't want the rest of you to feel left out." Or me picked on, I thought gratefully. "Joel, do you think you'd fall off the stage or run into everybody if you took off your glasses?"

"No," Joel said, in his usual shutting-out voice.

"Sure? You sound doubtful. Don't do it if it will make you uncomfortable. After all, Socrates was supposed to have worn some kind of glasses."

"It's okay. I'm getting contacts anyway." I don't know why he had a thing about his glasses, but I knew how he felt. I smiled at him. He looked at me as though I were a spot on the floor and started to walk off the stage.

"Just a minute, Joel. I haven't dismissed you. Sally, speak up more. Ted, try to put more expression in your lines. At the moment you might just as well be reading the weather report. All right, everybody, rehearsal tomorrow here at four. Be on time." She started to walk off the stage.

I found my voice. "Does that mean I'm to do the part of the queen permanently?"

Miss Ainslie stopped. "Don't you want to?"

Yes I did. "Sure, Miss Ainslie. But—" I took a breath. "You said I was too fat."

"I didn't exactly say that. But do as I suggested about your weight. For your own sake. You can, you know."

That again, and again, and again.

Sally and I walked out together.

"You have to have a prescription for those diet pills, don't you?" I asked.

"Yes. Won't your family doctor give you one?"

"Dr. Hastings? You've got to be kidding. He's so anti-pill—*any* pill—that he won't give anybody anything. Once, Mother called him up because I had a really lousy headache. I had taken an aspirin, but it didn't do any good. I think Mother wanted him to write me some fancy prescription, but he wouldn't. Instead, he told her to rub my back, it might relax me."

"Did she?"

"As a matter of fact, she did."

"Did it relax you?"

"Yes." I started to giggle as I remembered the scene. "But with every stroke she muttered something about Dr. Hastings being an old fuddy-duddy, miles behind the times, a mere tool of the AMA."

The whole scene, which till this moment I had forgotten, replayed itself in my mind. Father was passing my bedroom, saw us and stopped in the doorway. I could see him but Mother couldn't. She just kept on muttering. After a minute he started to grin. "You look like a witch doctor invoking a spell."

Mother grinned back without breaking stroke. "How do you know I'm not?" And all three of us laughed. It was one of those moments when everything came together. But there weren't many of them.

"Well, if she thinks he's so old-fashioned, why does she still go to him?"

"Well, Father likes him, natch, being sort of out of the Ark himself. And we've always gone to him since I was born, practically. You know how it would be in a small place if we stopped going to him."

"Maybe your mother has another doctor for herself without telling anybody. Lots of women do. At least one of my aunt's friends who's a nurse says that."

"What a crazy idea! I don't think—" But at that moment I remembered something. Mother had once sent me to her room to find something in her dressing table drawer. As I pulled it open I noticed a couple of plastic bottles of pills. I had thought nothing about it at the time, or if I had I assumed they were The Pill. But it seemed to me now that the name of the doctor on the bottom of each label was not Hastings.

"Maybe you're right. In fact, I think you are."

"Maybe she has a diet pill, Mel. Heaven knows she's skinny enough. Maybe it's natural, or just will power. But maybe it isn't. Why don't you look?"

"I will. But if she has them, why hasn't she told me? She's at me all the time to lose weight. It's her favorite subject."

"I don't know. But haven't you noticed, a lot of adults operate that way? Don't do what I do, do what I tell you. Or maybe she's scared that your father or fuddy-dud doctor would get after her. Or maybe she feels guilty."

"Why didn't you tell me that you're going to do an important role in the school play?" Mother asked at dinner.

I knew, of course, that sooner or later she would find out. But I had hoped it would be later. Somehow, when Mother moves in on one of my projects, it stops being mine and starts being hers.

"I was getting around to it. And anyway, it's not an important role. It's a small one."

"What play and what part?" Father asked.

"Antigone," Mother said. "And she's—"

"I asked Melissa. I'm sure she can answer for herself."

That's the kind of thing that makes our dinners such a feast of fun.

"Queen Eurydice," I mumbled through several stalks of broccoli. I hate broccoli. I also hate zucchini, which we were having along with the broccoli. And there's not much that can be said for dried-out breast of chicken, either. Probably right now, Sally's family, the Mayhews, would all be sitting down to pot roast, roast potatoes and gravy, with maybe green peas for a vegetable.

The scene leaped to my mind in technicolor and with a sound track: *Sally darling, have some more potatoes. We must build you up before the play. You know boys don't like skinny girls. They like girls with curves, like your friend, Melissa. Have some more gravy or one of these hot rolls with butter . . .*

"WILL YOU ANSWER ME. . . !" yelled my father.

"Sorry, Daddy. I was thinking of something else. What was it you were asking?"

"He was asking you, Mel—"

"I can carry my own ball, thank you," snapped Father. "I simply wanted to know if you liked the play and what you made of it. Why can't you pay attention for more than five minutes?" I could see Father's fork pushing a piece of broccoli around and around his plate. "Why the blazes do we have to have rabbit food night after night? This dinner is uneatable."

"Right on," I muttered. I was also glad that Father's attention had been diverted from the play. But not for long.

"Those are organically grown vegetables," Mother said. "And you should be grateful that there's not a drop of saturated fat on this table, since it is *men* who seem to suffer strokes and heart attacks in a ratio of five to two over women, although considering the degree of male exploitation—"

"She's off," Father said grimly.

"And furthermore," Mother went on, her voice raised, "I am trying to establish a pattern of healthful appetite, weight control and appropriate eating in Melissa to counter-influence her overcompensatory neurotic predilection—"

"You must have been talking to Claire," I said, but I was beginning to feel sick.

"Is that why Melissa gets up in the middle of the night and raids the refrigerator?" Father asked.

I was looking at the broccoli on my plate. I had nibbled off the tops; all that was left now was the stalks, a couple of small ones that didn't matter and a large one.

"She does *not*," Mother said. "Do you, Melissa?" I thought about the snack I had had the night before around two A.M.

"No."

"Then what were you doing downstairs?" Father asked.

"Looking up *Antigone* in that *Companion to Literature*

of yours. I thought it might give me some leads. Miss Ainslie—she's the drama coach—says we should work out our interpretations ourselves."

The lie was as easy as falling off a log, and in a strange sort of way, the moment I told it it became the truth. I had read the piece on *Antigone* in the *Companion*. Only the time shifted in my mind from yesterday afternoon to the middle of last night.

"I didn't know hunger for knowledge kept you awake," Father said. He can be hateful.

I went back to staring at my broccoli stalk.

Sometimes, when my loving parents start hacking at each other, a little door opens in my mind and I slip through it, like *Through the Looking Glass*. When I do, whatever's going on shuts off. It's neat. But occasionally it's hard coming back. Right now, what with the fracas over what I should eat, that little door opened of its own accord. If the broccoli stalk just had legs it would look like a praying mantis. Then I wouldn't have to eat it. I had seen one in the biology lab at school. The trouble is, I hadn't been prepared for it. I just walked into the lab to get a book I had left there, and there the thing was, on top of a white metal table. It looked like something out of a bad dream. I gave a kind of a squeak. The biology teacher came out of his little office. "What's the matter?" he asked.

I pointed to the praying mantis.

"Oh, that's Herbert. Come over and meet him. He's very gentle and an important part of nature's balance. He eats plant-destroying insects."

So I met Herbert and came to know him, if not to love him. But this broccoli stalk made me think of Herbert before he became a friend and was still a monster. Did he have feelings?

"Eat your broccoli, Melissa," Mother said, breaking through my meditations on Herbert.

"Why can't you at least have hollandaise sauce?" Father asked.

"I've just told you. Because of Melissa."

I tried on my new title: Fatsy Melissa, Preventer of Pleasant Eating. Nice. Herbert, the broccoli stalk, was still looking at me. Or perhaps Mrs. Herbert. And then, out of absolutely nowhere, the awful illustration in the anatomy book laid itself across the plate.

Through it all came Father's voice. "Well, I can only say that whatever it is you're trying, it isn't working. Every time I look at Melissa she seems to have put on five pounds. She—"

And then, without warning, something absolutely dreadful happened. My whole stomach rushed upward. I was sick all over my plate (alas, poor Herbert!) and my lap and I couldn't seem to stop. In the midst of it I wondered if it were some kind of punishment for my lie, because the box of cookies I had devoured in the middle of the night (plus another box this afternoon) were surely coming up.

"Oh, my God!" my father said. He leapt up, took one look and stalked out of the room.

I had certainly put an end to our dinner.

After that, I ran upstairs and was sick again.

"Ninety-nine," Dr. Hastings said about an hour later, taking the thermometer out of my mouth. "That's not too bad. You could run that much out of excitement alone." He wiped the thermometer off and put it back in its case and into his breast pocket. "What have you been eating, Melissa?"

"Everything, from the looks of it," Mother said. She was standing at the end of my bed. I felt terrible, but it was my soul that hurt, much more now than my stomach.

"What did you have for dinner?" the doctor asked.

"I'm very careful about our menus," Mother said, unconsciously smoothing the long sweater over her slacks and flat stomach. I watched her out of my half-shut eyes. "We had organically grown low-calorie vegetables, broccoli and zucchini—" I saw the doctor wince slightly at the word "organically"—"salad with lemon dressing and chicken. Although from the looks of what Melissa—well, it was obvious she'd been gorging on a lot of carbohydrate trash." Mother took a deep breath. "I am trying my best to get Melissa to—"

"Do you like organically grown broccoli and zucchini, Melissa?" Dr. Hastings asked, going towards the bathroom to wash his hands.

I shook my head which quite genuinely hurt.

Mother raised her voice. "That's hardly the point, Dr. Hastings. Melissa has to do something about her eating habits. I have read everything I can lay my hands on on the subject of obesity and—"

"Shall we continue the conversation downstairs?" Dr. Hastings said, coming out of my bathroom. "Melissa, I want you to drop by my office next week after school."

"Just tell me the day, Dr. Hastings," Mother said. "I'll bring her myself."

"No need for that. It's on her way home. Okay, Melissa?"

"Okay," I muttered, trapped.

"Any day'll do. Afternoons are my regular office hours and I shouldn't keep you waiting too long."

"I'd like to come with her, Doctor, so I can—" but Mother found herself talking to air. I could hear the doctor's feet going down the stairs. Mother ran after him. I got up, closed the door, pushed a chair in front of it and under the knob (there's no key; Mother confiscated it after a fight we had when I locked her out), went over and opened the window and went back to bed.

But I couldn't go to sleep. My head really throbbed. The sheets felt hot. Now I felt empty and hungry. I was fairly certain Mother would be back wanting to come in. From my bed I could see the steeple of St. Mary's Church at the front edge of Bunkerdom. It's the newest, largest and ugliest church in the suburb. Mother once said it was built by a lot of Irish *arrivistes* and that money breathed from every tile, negating the entire spiritual concept of life.

Father said she was a woolly-minded snob.

Mother said she supposed his secretary was a Catholic.

I've forgotten what went on after that.

Anyway, there it was, its floodlit steeple rising higher even than the Power and Light Building. For some reason it made me think of Ann O'Faolin and her father. . . . I heard Mother's steps coming back up the stairs. She came to the door. There was a pause. "Melissa?"

I lay very quiet.

"Melissa?" There was a soft rap on the door.

After a while she went away.

I looked at the luminous dial on my bed stand clock. Nine ten. The library would still be open. If I ran I could get there in ten minutes. Very quietly I got up, groped around for my jeans, sweater and poncho. Then I put on some sneakers. It was all deliciously simple. I got out of my window onto the garage roof, crossed that to the other end, slipped my leg over the trunk of the big oak and climbed down. I'd done this once or twice before, just for fun. But never at night, or only once, on Halloween when I heard the neighbors starting on another round of trick or treating and I knew Mother wouldn't let me go out again.

But the whole roof thing just shows how illogical adults are. Before Mother and Father go to bed they lock every window downstairs, the basement door and both the front door and the back door. It's never occurred to them that with the tree and the garage there they might as well leave the whole place wide open. And I'm not about to tell them. . . .

Ten minutes later I was walking into the library.

Five

When I saw Tremendous Teddy off to one side with *la belle* Claire, I almost wished I'd stayed in bed. But I hadn't. So I sauntered into the stacks, avoided that anatomy book that was out of place again, and found myself in the fiction section. There were all sorts of books there I should read— at some time in the future: *War and Peace*, *The Magic Mountain*, *Crime and Punishment*, plus some contemporary stuff. But what I took out was an old favorite of mine, a book of Spanish fairy tales. I tucked it under my arm so that the title wouldn't show and went back to the reading room.

Fairy tales are considered kid stuff at school and are officially frowned on as encouraging escape from reality. Mother says they are damaging to the psyche, and the psychiatrist she once sent me to said they represented a primal regression to the mythic presomething-or-other stage. I may not have the words right but that was the general idea. As a matter of fact, I really enjoyed the three sessions I had with him. For one thing, I went into New York alone on the train (he *ordered* Mother not to come in with me) and for another I made up some absolutely gorgeous dreams for him. Whenever he asked some stupid question I didn't want to answer, I'd hand him a dream. The first I handed him was quite true and rather uninteresting, something about a dog and the local pet show and a strange-looking man who was running it—not a bit like Mr. Hobbs, who really runs it. But I could see the doctor didn't like that dream, so the next time he asked me something boring I said it reminded me of another dream I had had—just to move off the subject—and he said "What?" So I had to make one up. This time it was in technicolor and the more I invented the more fascinating it got, and then the session was over. So I did this for the other two sessions and he got more and more excited and tugged at his collar and his earlobe until one snapped open and the other got crimson and I really had a good thing going. Then, whammo!—Father found out I was seeing a psychiatrist and Armageddon was on. I split during that as soon as Mother and Father got so involved they forgot to notice I was there. As I was softly closing the front door I heard Mother shriek "I suppose Miss Pierce doesn't approve of Freud!"

Since Miss Pierce is Father's secretary and such a large part of our family life I've often thought I should meet her, maybe ask her to lunch and secretly drop poison into her fruit cup from the Borgia ring I would then be carrying. But what with one thing and another I haven't got around to that.

Anyway—back to the library: I opened the book of Spanish fairy tales, plunged in, and a sort of lovely peace stole over me, only that isn't the right description. It started somewhere deep in my middle and worked out. And that was the last I remember until I finally became aware of a noise. I looked up.

The noise was made by a drunk who was being hauled to the door by Tremendous Teddy. "I'm not doing any harm," I heard him yell.

"Yes you are. You're molesting people and you snore and you smell," Teddy said loudly, pushing him towards the front door. "And if you don't go quietly I'll call the cops."

The wretched man sort of gargled something about not meaning to offend, but at that moment he was propelled through the front door.

For some reason it bothered me, maybe because anybody Ted was against I was for. I wondered if I would have helped him push the drunk out if we'd been on the old basis, and then I was really shaken, because I knew I would. It would have seemed like an act of civic virtue. Now it seemed like an act of bullying, and the difference had nothing to do with the drunk: it was how Teddy was treating me. Weird. No, not weird. But something that I couldn't quite get my finger on. I wondered what Miss Peabody would say. And I also wondered why Mrs. Summers was allowing it. I peered past some heads towards the librarian's desk. Just as I should have guessed, it was not Mrs. Summers, but her lame-brain stand-in, Miss Caldwell, who was watching the whole thing with her usual troubled, inept gaze.

She bustled over as Ted came back through the door and hurriedly whispered at him.

"It's okay, Miss Caldwell," Teddy said quite audibly. "He was bothering Claire."

Miss Caldwell went into another hurried whisper and then trotted back on the spike heels she still wears.

Ted tenderly helped Claire to her feet and they left the library. I guess after her trying sexual experience, Claire wanted the kind of consolation you couldn't give in the public library.

I went back to the fairy tales, but not for long. Miss Caldwell, looking as though she were summoning cattle from several pastures away, rang the bell that meant closing time.

I debated checking the fairy tales out against Mother finding them in my room and starting another hassle about my retarded reading habits. I could always put them in my underwear drawer. The word "drawer" started another train in my mind.

Did Mother have some of those pills Sally mentioned? I tried to remember if Mother had always been thin, and then, out of nothing, there sprang the memory of a wedding picture—Mother's and Father's. I hadn't seen it for years, not since I was about ten or eleven, and I wouldn't have seen it then if I hadn't been rummaging through a box of old photographs in the attic. I immediately took it downstairs to show Mother. But she didn't react at all the way I had expected. She said it had to go right back upstairs. All the way back up the three flights of stairs I kept trying to find out why she was mad and she wouldn't tell me. All she did say, which made no sense to me at the time, was "After all the trouble I've gone to to erase that Daisy June image!"

"Who's Daisy June?" I asked, as Mother put the photograph in an old chest we keep in the attic and locked it.

"Nobody you know," Mother said, putting the key in her pocket.

But I felt cheated and baffled. I had registered that Mother looked decidedly plump, but it didn't interest me. Of absorbing interest was the handsome, smiling man in uniform beside her. I knew it was Father and yet it was like looking at someone I'd never seen.

"Father looked different," I said, as Mother shepherded me out of the attic.

"We all looked different then. Time passes. Things change. Besides, Melissa, you've never seen him in uniform. It does great things for a man."

But it wasn't the uniform and, anyway, Mother was wrong. I had seen him in uniform once. It was the night of some kind of military affair in New York, and he came downstairs in his Air Force blues and wearing all his medals. I thought he looked splendid. But it was still not the way he looked in the picture and I tried to tell Mother this.

"Look, Melissa. I don't want to discuss it. And what were you doing up there anyway?"

As a matter of fact, I had gone up to read some of the fairy-tale books that Mother had insisted on taking out of my room and putting up there. I think she would have thrown them away, except they came to me from Father's mother and she didn't dare.

"Were you reading some of those fairy stories?" she said.

I lied. "No. Of course not."

"What were you doing up there then?"

I had an inspiration and hung my head. "I was reading a paperback a kid at school lent me. All the kids are reading it."

Mother frowned. "Well, why do you have to read it up there?"

"It's about sex," I said in an abashed way.

"Melissa, I've told you again and again that it is perfectly all right for you to read about sex. In fact, I've tried to talk to you about it before. It's high time you showed some curiosity. You're terribly backward about the whole subject. Where is the book?"

Fortunately, I had seen that question coming. "I tore it up in little pieces and threw it down the john. It—didn't have a proper cover and was only a few pages. But it had drawings, and I was afraid you'd see them. Sally's mother was furious when she saw them." I reminded myself to prime Sally as soon as possible in case the mothers decided to get together. But I could see right away it wasn't necessary.

"Well, that was very wrong of you, Melissa, not only because it can block up the plumbing, but because it shows you obviously have some kind of unhealthy, neurotic, puritanical guilt on the whole subject. I can't *think* where you get it."

I allowed myself to look neurotically guilty. It was better than another lecture on the danger of escapist reading.

Now, five years later, I stared down at the fairy-tale

book on the library table in front of me. Still clear as a color slide in my mind as my father's face in the wedding photograph, full of something I had never seen there. But I could also now see my mother. Maybe the wedding dress didn't become her, but whatever it was, she looked *dowdy*. Her shape, especially beside Father's lithe height, was a slightly thinner version of my own. And her hair was *brown*—just like mine.

What all this told me was that Sally must be right. Mother wasn't always thin. The pills in her drawer fell into place. What nerve!—to starve me out when she knew an easier way!

I didn't need the fairy tales. I put them back in the stacks and left the library. As I reached the bottom step I saw Teddy coming towards me from the common. My heart skidded.

"Where'd you come from?" I asked.

"The Shoppey. Wanna walk home? I'm on my way."

"No thanks."

"Why not? You shouldn't be out so late on a school night, anyway. Your folks know you're here?"

"Of course. I'm studying for a special project in the library. That was a neat act of charity you did, throwing out that poor old drunk. Big brave Teddy."

"If you like him so much, you can have him. Why don't you take him home with you? He's across the street. Passed out on a bench."

I glanced over. Yes, there he was.

"I didn't know you were a friend of law and order," I said nastily.

"That dirty old man made a pass at Claire. Tried to put his filthy hand on her arm."

"Well, well. Sir Galahad himself. But couldn't you choose a dragon nearer your size? And besides, what if he did try to put his hand on Claire? He didn't mean any harm."

"How do you know? And anyway, that's not the point. And I'm not a friend of law and order. The trouble with you, Melissa, is, as I've said before—you're jealous. Nobody cares whether he tried to paw you or not. Besides, even he's not that drunk." And with these noble words my ex-hero pushed me aside and stalked in the general direction of home.

I sat down on the low wall that runs around the library and stared at my toes. After a bit some more footsteps came up and stopped. "Hi!"

I looked up. "Hi!"

It was Joel Martin. He sat down. "You look like you're composing a suicide note. What's all the tragedy?"

Whenever Joel asks something like that he sounds as though he couldn't care less what the answer would be. It doesn't encourage confidences.

"What's it to you?"

"Granted, not much."

We sat there in silence, Joel's presence inhibiting me from enjoying my misery to the fullest.

Finally he said, "I saw you talking to Ted MacDonald. Is that what's giving you heartburn?"

My old instinct to stick up for Ted at all costs reactivated. "Of course not. And anyway, who are you to criticize him?"

"If you mean no one should criticize anyone, then I agree with you, I shouldn't. Is that what you have in mind?"

He leaned back and plucked a grass blade from the edge of the library lawn. Fitting it between his thumbs he blew and emitted a screech.

"I wish I could do that," I said. It seemed so satisfying. Ted could do it, but even though I asked him, he never showed me how.

"Here. Like this." Joel took another blade and showed me how to put it between my thumbs, leaving a small air space on either side. "It's the same principle as an oboe or bassoon. Now blow!"

I blew. Nothing happened.

"Try again."

I tried again, and again. The third time, to my vast surprise, there was a small squeak, like an uncertain mouse.

"I did it."

"Sure. Just keep on practicing. There's another way you can make a noise, too. Fold your hands against each other like this." He clasped his hands, put his thumbs together and blew. A low, mournful sound came out. Then he moved the fingers of one hand and played a few notes that could have been, with a little imagination, "My Country 'Tis of Thee."

"How do you do that?"

He showed me. "But I think you ought to practice them one at a time, or you'll get discouraged. Stick to the grass blade first."

I practiced with the grass blade for a while and got to the point where every fourth or fifth blow would produce a squeak. I put the blade down on my leg. "It's not really that difficult. But Ted wouldn't show me how when I asked him."

"Well, if I make the obvious and intelligent response to that, you'll get into another huff. Why do you go on letting him slap you down? You must know it's masochistic. You should see your face sometimes. You look at him as though he hung the moon, and he looks at you as though you were a mess on the sidewalk. So you go around thinking that's what you are. I mean, do you *like* it?"

Father had made his satiric comments about Ted, Miss Peabody had had her say. No one had ever laid the truth out so horrendously. And it was the truth. I could see it as though I were watching it happening to somebody else, and it was more than I could take. Before I knew what was happening I was crying.

"Hey, Mel, I'm sorry! I didn't mean to upset you like that."

"Then why did you say that? You're always making sarcastic comments. I'm going home."

I couldn't stop crying, but I got up and started to run across the street that bordered the common.

"Mel! Wait!"

Joel caught up with me on the other side of the street.

"Go away!"

"No. I won't. Look, Melissa, I like you. Why do you think I'm saying this? I don't want to hurt you. I know how you feel. I don't want you to be hurt. Ted MacDonald isn't worth it."

"You have no right to say that. And anyway, didn't

you say no one should criticize anyone? Besides, I'm not interested in your opinion of me. You're just a . . . a nothing." Joel didn't say anything.

After a minute, a little sorry because he had been trying to comfort me, and he did say he liked me, I said, "Joel, I'm sorry. I didn't really mean it."

"Oh, yes you did. Maybe you're sorry you said it, but you meant it all right." (Where had I heard that before?) "If you're okay I'm going home."

"Joel—" But at that minute there was a loud groan from behind the bushes at the edge of the common. "What's that?"

Joel climbed over the fence and pushed through the bushes. After a minute I called, "Joel? What's the matter? Who is it?"

"It's just a drunk."

"That's funny. He was on the bench."

"Well, he must have moved, because he's here now."

With a slight struggle I got over the fence and wiggled through the bushes. On the other side Joel was bending over a sprawled figure. The common is fairly well lit and I could see that it was, indeed, the drunk from the library.

"What's the matter with him?" I whispered.

"He's passed out," Joel said. "He also seems to have knocked his head. There's blood on it."

"What shall we do?"

Joel stood up. "There's a telephone booth over there. Can you stay here a second while I call the police?"

"Why are you calling the police? I mean, he's not breaking any law, is he?"

"They'll take him to the emergency room at the hospital or maybe bring an ambulance. Apart from being drunk, he should have somebody look at his head."

"Oh. Okay. I'll stay."

Joel ran over to the booth, telephoned and came back. "Look, why don't you go on home? It's still not that late."

"Why? I mean, don't you want me to stay?"

"It's just that I thought you might not want to be here when the police come."

"What would be wrong about that?"

He shrugged. "Nothing. If you don't care."

At that point the drunk seemed to come to. "My head," he said.

"You'll be okay in a minute or so," Joel said, and his voice was kind and warm, the way it had been for a few seconds when I first started to cry and before I said hateful things to him.

"I wanna drink," the man said, and tried to sit up.

Joel kept him down with a hand on his shoulder. "Not right now. Later."

At that point the police car and an ambulance came up. Two cops and two attendants carrying a stretcher jumped out and came over. "Okay, Jonesy," one of the officers said cheerfully, and bent towards the man.

"Is that his name?" I asked, curious.

"We don't know. That's why we call him Jonesy."

"You've seen him before?"

"Sure. He's a regular. Every few weeks he goes on a binge and ends up here."

"But why is he here?" Old movies like *The Lost Weekend* and *I'll Cry Tomorrow* were doing reruns through my mind. "I mean, why isn't he on skid row in New York?"

"Skid row's anywhere," one of the men said. "Any-where's there's a drunk and a bottle."

By this time the two ambulance attendants had got Jonesy onto a stretcher and were carrying him towards the ambulance.

One of the cops got out a notebook. "And who are you?" he asked, looking towards me.

I told him.

"Any particular reason you're here?"

I remembered about the pushers that occasionally (according to rumor) haunt this area. "I just came out of the library a few minutes ago."

"The library closes at ten. It's now ten forty. What have you been doing since? And you too, Joel?"

"We've been talking," Joel said quickly. "We're in the play at school and we're studying our parts together."

The policeman looked at Joel. "Okay," he said. "But I think it's time you both went home. Thanks for calling, by the way."

"He sounded like he knew you," I said to Joel as the ambulance and police car drove off.

"He does. Since it's so late I'll see you home. Let's go."

We walked along in silence. I kept trying to think of some way I could make it up to Joel for saying what I did. But that just reminded me more than ever of my refusal to believe Father. Without thinking, I let out a sigh.

"Now what?"

"Joel, you may not believe this, but right before school my father said something horrible to me, the way I did to you, and then apologized. And I said what you said to me, that I didn't think he was really sorry. And now I feel like a creep. Because I *am* sorry. Please forgive me."

Then Joel burst out, "It just bugs me that you go around begging to be accepted by—well—insensitive types who never will."

"Like Ted."

"Yes. Like Ted. You can put it down to jealousy or anything else if you want. But if you could just get over your addiction to being rejected by him you'd see what I mean."

"You mean if I seemed to like someone else and paid no attention—"

"You can just cut that masterly thought right there. I'm not about to play dummy decoy for your trap."

We had reached my door.

"Good night," Joel said, and turned back down the path.

"Good night."

As I mooched over to climb up to the garage roof I really felt rotten.

Six

I put Sally's suggestion into operation the next morning.

While Mother was downstairs I sneaked into her bedroom and opened her dressing table drawer. Sure enough, there were two phials of pills. One contained white tablets and was obviously a sleeping pill because the prescription said to take at bedtime. The other contained orange and blue capsules, the kind with thousands of multicolored thingies inside that keep going off all day. The name of the doctor on both labels was Butler. I'd never heard of him, and I did know that he couldn't be Mother's gynecologist because his name is Morrison and he's a friend of Dr. Hastings. Also, the drugstore label looked different from the one everybody uses in the village. I peered at the small, blurred print. Miller's Pharmacy, and the address was in the next town.

My sense of grievance increased. So Mother was sneaking off getting thin pills from some secret medico while she expected me to lose weight on will power. I took a couple out of the bottle and flitted back to my bathroom.

Just as I was about to swallow one, the thought dawned that the pill might be for something else altogether. I stared down at it, wondering how I could find out. Of course I could always take it off to the local drugstore and ask. But if the druggist on duty were old Mr. Lowenstein himself, he'd want to know where I got it and what I was going to do with it, and I wouldn't put it past him to phone Mother. Mr. Lowenstein is the right-is-right-and-wrong-is-wrong and okay-kids-that's-enough-noise and quiet-down-or-I'll-call-the-cops type. But one of the boys in my class, Jim Macy, jerks sodas and helps behind the counter there after school. He'd tell me. I debated for a minute, caution fighting against desperation. After all, even if the pill were for something else, what harm could one do me? I put the capsule in my mouth and swallowed it with some water. If it took away my appetite, great. If it didn't, then I'd know it was for something else.

I dressed and went downstairs to breakfast, wishing that I could skip the whole thing and sneak out to school without seeing anybody, since memories of what happened last night at dinner were not doing anything for my ego. But the hassle it would cause was not worth it.

I realized shortly after I slid onto my chair at the kitchen breakfast table that I would probably never have to ask Jim about the pill. It was obviously a diet pill and it was working before I finished my breakfast. I had attacked my bowl of cereal and milk with my usual ravenous enthusiasm, but by the time I was through that I was full, which was unheard of. Normally it took at least two pieces of toast or an egg and toast and a glass of milk before I could totter off to school. That is, if Mother weren't there to nag me out of half of it, in which case I had to make it on less.

Mother was watching me. "How do you feel this morning, Melissa?"

"Fine," I said, and I did. A warm tide of well-being was flowing through me, neutralizing the embarrassment and humiliation I felt whenever I thought of the scene at dinner the night before.

"Where's Father?" I asked casually.

"He went into town early this morning." Mother poured herself some tea and put the teapot down. Mother's breakfast consists of cranberry juice, brewer's yeast and tea, a combination I tried once, at Mother's insistence, and found gaggy and inadequate. I wondered now if she took the pill as soon as she got up.

"Did he say anything about last night?" I ventured.

"That was our main topic of conversation, if you can call it that. You know how your father is in the morning."

I knew that probably meant that Mother wanted to talk about it and Father didn't. "Was he worried that I might be ill or something? Like the beginning of a brain tumor?"

"No, Melissa. After everything you upchucked he wasn't worrying about a brain tumor. More like—" she stopped.

"Like what?"

Mother got up and took her glass and cup to the sink. "Don't ask."

"That's worse than anything, Mother. It makes it sound hideous."

Mother didn't say anything.

"Tell me what Father said." Awful as it was, I had to know.

Mother turned around. "His words were, 'Melissa's problem is compulsive, pathological greed.' Does that make you feel better?"

No. I tried to field the words in some part of me where they wouldn't hurt so much. But that didn't work. While I was doing this I noticed that Mother was angry, too. I could tell by the lines running down beside her nostrils and the straight thin look her lips have when she's mad. Was she angry at Father? No, every nerve in me was registering that her hostility was directed at me.

I asked carefully, "How come you've stayed so thin ever since I can remember, Mother? You weren't thin in that wedding picture. I mean, was it all just will power?"

"Yes. It was. And that's what you're going to have to learn. I wasn't that much older than you, maybe seven years, and I did it on will power."

What a cool liar.

"No pills, no nothing," Mother said, refuting waves from my mind. She turned around and started unloading the dishwasher from last night.

Of course I could whip out the second pill I had wrapped up in a tissue in my jeans pocket and confront her with it. But where would that get me, except in worse trouble than ever and no pill to help me out? At this point I was technically, if not in the clear, at least not breaking the law. No one had said I couldn't take the diet pill. If I wanted to keep my supply going, I'd better keep my trap shut.

I got up and picked up my books. "I'm late. Sorry about Father." And I walked out of the kitchen, picked up my poncho in the hall and left the house.

My head really felt funny the rest of the day. Sometimes I nearly jumped out of my skin. Other times a lovely euphoric cloud surrounded me and kept out all the slings and arrows. It did worlds for my self-esteem. I made lots of funnies in class and in the halls between classes and stopped being afraid of whether people would laugh at me.

That afternoon I was feeling particularly ept and couth because I'd had one half grapefruit and a cup of black coffee for lunch—*solamente,* as our Spanish teacher would say. Those little rainbow bitsies dissolving inside me all day were really doing their thing. At lunch I felt positively high, at least what I guess is high from the descriptions I've heard and read, because I've never actually experienced it. It was a little scary, truth to tell, and my heart was pounding as though I had played a full half of field hockey, but I didn't want to eat. And not eating was where it was at. Maybe by the time I had shrunk my stomach and lost weight I'd have some kind of a brake on my pathological compulsive greed, or was it compulsive pathological? The words had been in my mind all morning, behind everything else. And they hadn't been just words as words—a visual ripple of letters. They were sounds, knife-edged, pointed, sinewy, a judge's sound coming from my father's throat.

> "I'll be judge, I'll be jury,"
> Said cunning old Fury;

"I'll try the whole cause,
And condemn you to death."

The fearsome little verse from *Alice in Wonderland* flowed in and out of my ears through class.

My father, of course, was not a judge. Not yet. He was a lawyer, an advocate. An advocate for whom? Advocate . . . adversary. I was the advocate, pleading for myself. He was the adversary. . . .

"MELISSA!"

I jumped. It was the English class, last of the day, and my mind had been turned off. I could feel my stomach flatten into my backbone, but I still wasn't hungry, which made up for the headache and the queer, bright, unfocused feeling in my head, and the fantasies, the sweat that suddenly broke out on my face and body.

"Yes, Miss Peabody?" I tried to sound casual.

"I've spoken to you three times. Are you all right?"

I could hear the concern in her voice. Wasn't it just my luck that it came from a tacky, middle-aged, unattractive schoolteacher, not Ted, not my father, not even my poor, irritating, silly mother.

Anger rode back on an up wave. I felt invincible.

I leaned forward. "I'm just fine, Miss Peabody. But are *you* all right?"

She could have turned it around with one of her lightning comebacks and the joke would have been on me. But for a fatal second she paused. As the laugh I had gone after broke out, our eyes met. There was something in hers that made me feel small—a kind, calm knowingness. We had always been sort of friends, she and I, and now I had served her up to the lions. Well, she shouldn't have made me jump.

But she said amiably, "I, too, am just fine, Melissa. Sorry to disturb your dreams. I hope they were productive ones."

To my relief, the bell rang. "Homework," Miss Peabody said, and started assigning it.

I wondered if she'd keep me after class. But she went trudging out, her arms full of books, her sweater on crooked.

"She should really give herself to the thrift shop," Miss Thirty-five-cashmere-sweaters said. "I mean, it's *sad*. Imagine looking like that and having a life like that."

Yes, I thought. Imagine.

"How do you know what her life's like?" Joel asked, walking past. "For all you know she may be a poet, a mystic, even a lover."

"You've simply got to be kidding," Claire Reynolds chimed in, tossing back her hair.

"Why? Because she doesn't look like Miss Clairol?"

Tremendous Teddy ranged up, muscles bulging. "Why don't you keep your big mouth shut, or I'll split it open for you again."

It seemed like a perfectly ordinary Ted MacDonald all-American kind of a comment, his usual method of taking care of almost any situation. And I expected Joel's sarcastic tongue to slice him to bits. Even Ted, through the token bluster, looked guarded.

But Joel's tongue failed him. Instead of annihilating the clan MacDonald, he went red, and reddest of all was the scar running through the center of his upper lip.

"Say, somebody did open it up before! How about that?" Miss Cashmere said.

Claire's sapphire eyes narrowed. "I once saw a scar exactly like that. It was on a kid who'd had a harelip."

Ted grinned happily. "Well, well. So that's it."

Joel was white now, all except his scar, which was still red and sticking out like a high-voltage cable. "How come you know, Claire? Or was that one of your father's botched specials? When he's practicing on charity patients, I mean." Since Dr. Reynolds had indeed had a bit of legal unpleasantness with a badly scarred charity patient on whom he had done some plastic surgery, the discussion might have gone anywhere, including the hospital and the morgue, if Ann O'Faolin hadn't stuck her head in.

"The play is supposed to be rehearsing now, in the theater, on the double."

Since my only speech was at the very end of the play, I went and sat down halfway back to watch the others. Miss Ainslie got Ann and Sally—playing Antigone and her sister Ismene—and the chorus up onto the stage, and the rehearsal started.

I'd never had much to do with Miss Ainslie, who had come to the school in the middle of the previous year trailing a fair amount of publicity. Why, after English repertory and Broadway, she should end up coaching high school drama in Westchester, I couldn't imagine. You'd think she would have at least gone on to some place like Vassar or Radcliffe. Whatever the reason, I began to realize as I watched her that their loss was certainly our gain. Not that I hadn't heard she was good. After last year's *As You Like It*, which was talked about for weeks and even mentioned by one of the New York papers, I shouldn't have been surprised. But I had never seen her work before.

Ann, as Antigone, was good. Sally, as Ismene, wasn't at first, despite her early good reading. Maybe it was nerves or playing opposite the almost professional Ann. Whatever the cause, Sally had stiffened up but, as Miss Ainslie went through the lines with her again and again, she started to loosen and sound human once more. It was like magic. And Miss Ainslie herself, up on the stage, going through the part with her was different. She was like Ann in that she came alive. She wasn't really tall, but she looked tall; she wasn't really good-looking, but what came over, somehow, was an enormous attractiveness, a sort of power that compelled out of me something I didn't even know I had.

I was so engrossed, watching her, that it wasn't until she turned her attention to the chorus, huddled in a lump to one side of the stage, that I noticed Joel was missing. Ted, with Claire, of course, beside him, was sitting in the front row along with the two boys playing the guard and the blind prophet. With those on the stage and me that comprised the entire cast, except for Joel, who had the largest role.

"Where's Joel?" Miss Ainslie said from the stage.

No one knew.

"Well—go find him. We'll need him in about five minutes." She turned back to the chorus.

"He knew we were going to rehearse. Why can't he get himself here?" Ted muttered.

I stood up. "I'll go."

I wasn't sure why I offered, whether it was to help Joel or to help Miss Ainslie.

"Be sure and look in the boys' locker room," Ted said helpfully. Claire giggled.

I went outside and bumped into Joel coming up the steps.

"Miss Ainslie's looking for you."

"I figured it'd be about now." His dark hair looked wet around his temples and forehead and instead of the shirt he'd had on before he was wearing a dark blue turtleneck sweater. It clung to him and it occurred to me that in a skinny way he had a nice build.

"Where've you been?" I asked. "Swimming?"

"No."

I noticed his mouth then. The scar was white again, almost invisible.

Joel was watching me. "If I dunk it in ice-cold water or hold an ice cube against it, the red fades."

I was dying to know whether he had had a harelip or not, but I was determined not to ask. But the effort so inhibited me I couldn't think of anything else to say. I finally settled for, "We'd better go back."

He came up beside me. "Yes. It was a harelip. The scar always gets red when I get upset, or very tired." We started to walk back into the theater. He said in his indifferent voice, "I thought I had got over being sensitive about it. I guess I haven't."

I stopped at the door. "You're right about Ted. He's a crumb. Even if he isn't in love with me, you'd think we'd still be friends, after all these years. But in front of other people—"

"He does it to impress Claire."

"Yes. I know. Thanks, by the way, for sticking up for Miss Peabody."

He looked at me curiously. "Why did you make fun of her, then, if you like her?"

The truth was, I felt different now from the way I did in class an hour or so ago. I was flying then, but my capsule must have been running low because now I was feeling let down and flat. "I guess I was showing off."

"Anything for a little popularity."

I turned around and walked back in and sat in my seat halfway back. I can't stand sarcasm.

As soon as Joel came through the door Miss Ainslie said, "There you are. Come on up. I want to rehearse you and the chorus and—" She peered into the auditorium again. "Tim, the guard, you come up, too."

At the end of an hour Miss Ainslie said in exasperation, "Joel, what's happened to you? Your voice is good, but you're speaking the part as though it were the logarithm table. What is your mind on? The square on the hypotenuse?" There were appreciative giggles from below.

"A square thinking about a square," came from some wit in the first row.

"Look," Joel said. "You picked me for the part. I didn't ask for it. You want it back? You can have it." And with that he tossed the text he was holding at Miss Ainslie and started to walk off the stage.

"Pick that up at once, Joel. Never throw a book. *Never.* If you're unable to appreciate its contents, then take up comic books or stickball."

There was an all-around silence, resulting from surprise as much as anything else: surprise at the crackling authority that no teacher had dared use for I don't know how long, surprise that it was Joel up there playing Danny the

Red. *Joel*. Maybe he was working to change his image. If he won this title he would certainly no longer be Mr. Foureyes Blah.

But he didn't. After a minute he stooped and picked up the book and handed it to the drama coach.

"Keep it and try again," she said.

And he did. I didn't know whether to be glad or sorry. But from the sniggers from the chorus as well as from the auditorium, it was plain that he was back in his same old picture frame.

They tried again, first the Chorus of Theban Elders and then Joel as Creon in his long opening speech.

"Well," Miss Ainslie said when they were through, "the chorus still sounds like the junior glee club and Creon like the First National Bank laying out the rules for credit. And before the rest of you fall in the aisle laughing, let me tell you that you're no better. It doesn't sound to me as though any of you had the faintest memory of what I told you the play was about."

Nobody spoke. Ann seemed miles away. Sally looked scared. Finally Ted cleared his throat. "You said it was about civil rights and the state."

"And what else?"

Joel had been staring at his feet. But he raised his head and said, "Hubris."

"Yes. Hubris. Do you remember what that means?" She looked around and finally back to Joel. "Well. Joel, what does it mean?"

"Pride. Arrogance."

"Yes. You could even call it determined self-will. Everything's going to be done my way. According to Greek belief, any man or woman who was guilty of hubris was punished by the gods. But his punishment grew out of his own act. And the Greeks believed in that kind of justice as profoundly as we believe that if you jump out of an eighteenth-story window you'll spread all over the pavement. Not because the police or the courts say so, but because you defied the law of gravity. Do you understand?"

It was an impressive speech, not just because of what she said, but because she said it with such passion.

"All right," she said abruptly. "That's all for today. We start rehearsal the same time tomorrow. And you had better show some understanding of your parts and how they relate to the central theme of the play. Or we'll choose some bubbly comedy to do."

And with that she walked off the stage into the wings.

It was some kind of tribute that the rest of us left without any wisecracks.

I was halfway across the school grounds when I remembered that I had left my books in the auditorium where I had been sitting. And I had to have them for homework. The flatness and depression that had lifted during the last half hour was back. Reality had returned, and reality made it clear I had to have the books before I went home.

The seating area of the auditorium was dark when I walked in, but the stage and footlights were on so that the entire stage was bathed in light. I stood there for a minute, almost expecting some of the characters, maybe Antigone and Ismene, to walk on and start to speak their lines. Somebody must have forgotten to turn off the stage lights, I thought, and groped my way down the side aisle and across the seats to where I had been sitting. But as I did I noticed a figure sitting a few seats from where I had been. After another minute, I realized it was Miss Ainslie, because she moved her head and I could see the twist she wears at the back.

"Who is that?"

"It's me, Miss Ainslie, Melissa."

"Oh. Come over here, child."

I can't describe her voice. It was different. Tired. Warm. Almost sad.

I went over. "Is something wrong?" she asked.

"No. I left some books here."

"Oh. I thought you were having second or third or even fourth thoughts about the play."

"No."

"I'm sorry we didn't get to go over your speech this afternoon, Melissa. I intended to take you at the end. But then—I got carried away, I guess."

"I—I liked what you said, Miss Ainslie. About hubris," I said, stricken with unusual shyness.

"Did you, Melissa? Why?"

I didn't really know. I groped around in my mind for a minute to see if I could catch the gut of whatever it was that satisfied me.

She put out her hand and clasped my arm. "You don't have to answer if you don't want to. I didn't mean to pry."

I couldn't have been more surprised. Miss Ainslie had always seemed, in a friendly way, rather aloof. She took her hand away.

"No, Miss Ainslie. It's not that. It's just that I'm not

sure. I think I liked what you said because it seemed to make some kind of sense—you know, cause and effect, justice coming out of effect."

"Well, remember it the next time you find yourself blindly determined to do something that you know in your heart is wrong," she said lightly, and got up. "I'll have to turn out the stage lights."

She went up on the stage, turned out the lights one by one and then turned on one auditorium light so we could get out.

I was thinking about what she said when she came down off the stage. She has a face like one of the John Singer Sargent paintings in the Metropolitan Museum in New York that Mother dragged me to once: high and proud and intelligent. I wondered how old she was. Not old, but also not young, and middle-aged seemed the wrong word. I wondered what Mother would say about her hair, which was dark blond with broad gray streaks and simply pulled back. Her figure wasn't as good as Mother's—anyway, not as fashionably skinny, yet there was something about her that made me wish I could be like her when I grew up.

"You're staring, Melissa," she said, smiling a little.

I could feel myself blush. "Sorry," I muttered and said hastily, "Were you sort of seeing the play on the stage when I came in?"

She flipped off the remaining light. "Yes. I like to do that. The confusions seem to unravel and the play, as it should be, comes clear. I get some of my best ideas that way."

We left the auditorium and started walking across the

school yard to the street. There was one more thing on my mind I wanted to get out.

"I'm going to lose weight," I blurted out.

"Good. Sensibly, I trust. No foolish fads. Does your mother approve?"

"Oh, yes. She's always been after me to lose weight."

"Then, if you yourself want to, it's unanimous. There's just one thing I want to emphasize." We had stopped where the path branched off to the administration building. "The reason I want you to lose weight is because you will look better and be happier about yourself up on a stage if you do. Not because I think you look awful. I don't. It's not a rejection thing, do you understand?"

Yes, I understood all the way down to my toes. Maybe it was because the pill was giving out, but it was all I could do to keep from crying. At that moment there was nothing in the world I wouldn't have done for her. But to keep from making a total fool of myself I just nodded. "Yes," I managed to get out.

"All right. See you at rehearsal tomorrow."

"What was Melissa supposed to see Dr. Hastings about?" Father asked that night at dinner, poking at the big potato that Mother had had Samantha, our cook, bake for him after his scathing comments about rabbit food and uneatable dinners.

Mother watched him put about half a stick of butter into it. "If that raises your cholesterol level and gives you a heart attack I want you to remember it's your own fault."

"That shall be my final thought as I join the choir invisible," Father said, mashing the butter in.

93

Evidently a few of those little thingies were still working inside me because while the potato looked good, not having it didn't make me feel utterly deprived, like a famine disaster victim. However, I knew Mother would have something memorable to say if she caught me eyeing the forbidden fruit, so I carefully kept my eyes away, even though not thinking about it was like going into a corner and not thinking about a hippopotamus. Impossible.

"Melissa and I are watching our figures," Mother said, smoothing the napkin over her lap.

Father grunted and the corners of his mouth turned down. Quite suddenly I wished that he would go away and stay away and not come back. It would make life so much easier. He and Mother wouldn't have these jabby little fights and I wouldn't feel like a bomb always on the point of exploding. I developed this further, making Father something romantic—like a New England sea captain, a sunnier Captain Ahab who came home on rare intervals and left again the moment everyone stopped being glad to see him. I was imagining him with a flat stovepipe hat, a beard and his peg leg, stumping down Maple Road. . . .

"Melissa! I asked you a question!"

I jumped, shooting a brussels sprout off the plate. "What is it, Father?"

"Why do you have to see Dr. Hastings?"

"Because I was sick last night," I mumbled, diving after the sprout.

Father's fine nostrils quivered. Sometimes I think he looks like a blend of Gregory Peck and Laurence Olivier, which just shows what a cross he is to bear, being good-looking like that.

"I should have thought that overeating is the main cause of most of your troubles."

"Like pathological, compulsive greed?"

He glanced quickly at Mother, who looked annoyed, and guilty. "That wasn't said for your ears, but yes."

I found myself thinking of what Miss Ainslie said. It was something warm to hold.

"And the cure for that, Melissa, is will power. All you have to do is make up your mind."

"Not everyone has a will of iron," Mother put in. "And you refuse to let me send Melissa to a psychiatrist."

"At fifty dollars an hour twice a week? You've got to be kidding."

"I daresay you spend that much, one way or another, the nights you stay in town," Mother said, nervously eating some of Father's potato, which was near her right hand, our dining room table, minus leaves, being rather small.

Father sat and watched her for a minute. Then he laughed. "All roads always lead to Rome, don't they?"

All of a sudden I'd had it with their bickering. "Why don't you two get a divorce?" I said. "Father can go and live in sin with Miss Pierce until they can get married. Mother can go back to New York and take up good works or being a secretary or whatever she was doing, and I can live in a commune where nobody cares how much I eat, or when, and nobody makes me feel like a freak."

Suddenly Father was towering over me. "How dare you speak to me like that? Who told you anything about Miss Pierce? Get up when I talk to you. Do you hear?"

I didn't move.

"Melissa!"

Mother said nervously, "You shouldn't . . ."

I got up and faced my father. "How dare you make me feel ugly and repulsive all the time? How dare you and Mother fight so much? How dare you be such rotten parents? Do you know kids my age are on drugs and are having pot parties and sex? Where have you been all the time? What kind of world do you live in down on Wall Street? Don't you know what's happening? Don't you ever do anything but go to bed with Miss Pierce?"

I saw Father's hand before it hit me. I could have ducked, but I didn't. I wanted him to hit me. It was the most real thing that had happened between us in years. I was vaguely aware that Mother was shrieking something. But I didn't pay any attention. I hated them both and wanted out. Right after his hand had smacked across my cheek, I cried, "I hate you" and split out the front door and ran.

Seven

I walked down into the village. But the first thing that I saw
was the Shoppey and I could see quite a few kids inside, although none of my own particular gang. I debated going in,
but as a great whiff of vanilla surrounded me when somebody came out, I knew I had better not. By this time I really
was hungry. In fact, I was starved. If I had thought about
Mother and Father and the gentle family get-together I had
just left, I would have marched straight in and eaten about
four hot fudge sundaes and one of their giant economy-sized
banana splits. So I kept pushing that scene away, and what I
used to push it away with was what Miss Ainslie had said. It
was about the nicest thing anyone had ever said to me and it
got better every time I thought about it.

I debated going to see Sally, but her family is pretty dreary about school nights and study. Besides, I really didn't want to talk to anyone, so to keep myself out of the Shoppey I went to a double-feature movie. It must have been some kind of revival because the first one was an old thirties or forties comedy and I laughed hysterically all the way through. The second was a five-handkerchief English World War II movie, my favorite type, and I cried and cried.

When I came out I felt better. I guess that's what movies like that are for. I had thought, of course, of running away altogether to that commune I was talking about, and maybe if the family brawl had occurred before today I would have. But Mother's pill and Miss Ainslie dragged me home. I wanted to get thin both for me and for Miss Ainslie, and I wanted to be in the play.

As I neared home I debated whether to walk through the front door or go up the garage roof. I really didn't want any more hassle. But if they were waiting up for me and discovered tomorrow morning that I had got in, that would be the end of my secret exit. I wouldn't put it past Father to put bars on my window.

So I marched up the path and through the front door, muttering to myself, *Half a league, half a league, half a league onward. Into the valley of death rode Melissa Hammond. Brave girl, stout fella, jolly good show,* and waited for the big guns of the enemy.

But there was no cannon's roar as I walked through the front door.

Bits of the English movie (properly adapted) went through my mind.

"The enemy seems very quiet, sir."

"Yes, Hammond. But that doesn't mean they've vanished. Take three men and reconnoitre."

"Very good, sir."

I stood in the hall. The house felt empty. Then I heard something that sounded halfway between a sniff and a sob and went into the living room.

Mother was sitting at one end of the sofa. On the end table beside her was the decanter of bourbon and a glass with about an inch left at the bottom. The decanter was almost empty.

Mother and I stared at each other.

"Well," she said. "I hope you're satisfied. Your father has packed a bag and gone. Just as you suggested."

"You mean to live with Miss Pierce?"

"He didn't announce that as his intention, but undoubtedly." She had a little trouble with that word. Then she said, "Among the other things your father threw at me was the accusation that I had told you about that . . . about Miss Pierce. He wouldn't believe I hadn't. So I want to know, how did you know?"

I shrugged. "That's easy. I heard you. You and Father aren't exactly quiet in your fights."

She swallowed what was left in her glass and poured the last of the bourbon into it. She took another swallow and sat staring at the glass. I waited for her to ask where I had been. But she didn't. What she did say was, "I suppose my conscience will flay me tomorrow for saying this to you, but right from the beginning you've been nothing for me but bad luck."

"Thanks a lot. I like you, too."

"Don't be impertinent."

"Impertinent? When you tell me that all I've been to you is trouble?"

Mother took a swig from her glass. "I didn't exactly shay—say that. I said from the beginning you were bad luck. And you were. It was because you were on the way that your father married me. You didn't know that, did you? You kids today think you're so liberated and we're such fogies. Well—your father married me because he had to. And I don't think he's ever forgiven me—or you."

Mixed with pain was relief. What Mother said made sense out of so much. But suddenly I remembered the wedding picture, and the way Father looked.

"He didn't look that way in the wedding picture, like he was being forced."

"He was making the best of a bad job. I think, for a while, he managed to talk himself into believing it was what he wanted. But it didn't last. I'll say this for your father, he may be a cold, arrogant so-and-so, but he doesn't kid himself about the way he feels or about what's going on." Mother gave a little hiccup and then started to cry into her handkerchief.

Vaguely I noticed that her mascara was running, and like a slide in front of her face with its black streaks and pink swollen eyelids, slid the picture of the drama coach. Mother and Miss Ainslie must have been about the same age, but it was like looking at a child and a woman.

The awful part was, I felt nothing except a desire to get upstairs and close myself into my bedroom.

So for Mother I was bad luck from the time I was conceived. You'd think I'd be mad or upset or something. But what I felt was free, at least as far as Mother was concerned. Because there's nothing so unfree as all love on one side (I'm doing this for you, darling, whether you like it or not). If I was bad luck for her, that was good luck for me, because I owed her nothing.

But Father was something else. I felt anger there and a desire to hurt him so strong that it made me dizzy.

I stood around for another minute. Mother was still crying. I knew I should go over and comfort her but I didn't want to. I didn't know why I didn't feel sorry for her, but I didn't. I think I would have for the girl in the wedding picture, but I couldn't for Mother. Finally I said, "I'm sorry, Mother," and went up to my bedroom.

I thought I was tired. Normally I'm asleep five minutes after I pull up the blankets. But I couldn't go to sleep. I kept seeing the empty decanter and Mother's mascara streaming down her face. Some of the kids at school talk a lot about how their parents are always loaded, but until tonight I've never seen it with mine. I've often seen them have drinks before dinner, and I know Mother likes it better than Father. In fact it was during a fracas about Mother's drinking at a party the night before that Mother had produced one of her better lines. "Your father," she said to me as though he were not there pretending to read the Sunday paper, "is the only person I know who is descended on all sides from Calvin Coolidge." Father laughed so hard at that that he lost his line of battle. Probably because Father was trying to hold the lid down, they never seemed to make the fertility rite out of drinking that some of the kids' folks do.

Should I go down and find the rest of the bourbon in the house and pour it down the sink, the way one girl swears she does with her father? Maybe I should, but I wasn't going to.

I turned over and tried to lull myself to sleep. What slid in front of my eyes this time was Father's handsome face. I could see his look of distaste. I wondered if Miss Pierce saw it. And then I was really awake. What was she like? Did Father look at her the way he looked at Mother in the wedding picture? I supposed she must be beautiful or terribly attractive and sexy. I tried to summon up a picture but it kept coming through looking either like Marlene Dietrich or Audrey Hepburn, depending on whether she was blond or dark. I tried to imagine either one sitting outside Father's office and saying "Mr. Hammond's office" every time the phone rang. How long had I known she was Father's girl friend? At one time, long ago, it had been kind of a family joke. But I couldn't remember when it had stopped being a joke and become real.

By this time my heart was pounding in an uncomfortable manner.

I got up and leaned over the bannister. There was no sound from below, but the light was still on in the living room. Softly I went into Mother's and Father's bedroom. I opened Mother's dressing table drawer and found the two containers. Luckily for me they were both almost full. I took four from each bottle and went back to my room. I swallowed a sleeping pill, put the rest in a tissue in my jeans pocket, set the alarm on my clock radio and was asleep almost immediately.

It was lucky about the alarm because I would certainly have overslept. Getting out of bed was like pulling myself out of a pool of molasses.

Mother wasn't up when I went into the kitchen. I went into the living room. The glass was there and the empty decanter plus a bottle of bourbon and an overflowing ashtray, which was a surprise. Father smokes occasionally, but Mother, on a health kick since I can remember, rarely takes a cigarette. The place stank of stale smoke. I debated cleaning it up and then decided against it, just in case Mother had forgotten what she'd been doing. I went back to the kitchen wondering if she'd bothered to remember that she could have burnt the house down, or that liquor was fattening. That led me to wondering what kind of figure Miss Pierce had. But thoughts like that went nowhere.

I had swallowed the diet pill before I came down so I was no longer hungry. I drank some instant coffee and ate half a grapefruit. I paused, wondering if I should go up and see if Mother was all right. But she might wake up then, and I didn't want to have to cope with her this morning.

It was all too much.

After that it was as though I had put my parents away into a drawer in my mind and locked it. It sounds crazy, but it made life much easier. Father wasn't there, of course, and Mother and I sort of revolved around each other like two galaxies whose paths never quite touched. Later, when it seemed impossible that we could live like this, I realized it was because we were both, for entirely different reasons, pretending that absolutely nothing had happened.

That night when I came home for dinner Mother said, very casually, "I'm sorry I wasn't quite myself last night."

"It's okay," I said, making for the stairs and my room.

"I trust I didn't say anything—well, anything that might have upset you."

That was really rare, I thought. I looked at her and realized she didn't remember. She was picking at a flower arrangement on the hall table. As I hesitated, she looked up at me and said, "That sweater's far too tight. I've told you and told you, when you're overweight, it's better to wear clothes that are loose. The rib-huggers are for people without midriff bulge." And her hand smoothed her own flat midriff.

I went upstairs and stole a few more of both kinds of pills. It was going to be a long haul.

One of the weird aspects of this whole period was that I stopped talking to people. I mean I stopped hashing over every last aspect of my daily life with Sally or Ann either on the phone or at school. For one thing, they were not only in the play, they were the leads. With Ann this had always meant that she turned off everything else. It wasn't that she was selfish or anything like that. It was just that you could see that whatever you were saying was just not penetrating —not until after the play was over. Sally turned out to be almost as bad. And of course, while we were all either in or watching rehearsal all our spare time, Sally, like Ann, was actually on stage. Who had time to talk?

There was another reason which is hard to explain, at least logically. But the whole pill thing was so tied up with the rest of the family mess—Mother's drinking, Father's absence—that I just didn't want to give anyone a chance to say, "How are things?" Somehow or other, by my not talking, it was being held together, contained.

Something else that happened shook me up. It occurred

about a month later while I was taking the pills out of Mother's drawer and copying down the prescription numbers. I had already realized I was going to have to replace the pills if I didn't want to be found out. Somehow I would have to get to that drugstore and pick up some more. Anyway, I was replacing the tops of the phials when a wish that both my parents would die and leave me alone forever absolutely took over my mind. It was so sharp and vivid that I wouldn't have been surprised if I found it had happened. I just stood there for a minute, and then it went away. I decided that, in addition to everything else, I must be truly wicked.

Mother never once mentioned Father, if she'd talked to him or had a letter from him. Since the mail came when I was at school I wouldn't know if there were a letter and of course I wouldn't know if they'd talked on the telephone. And I didn't ask.

We were having rehearsals every afternoon now, and since my part was at the very end, it gave me any excuse I needed to come home late for dinner. But I didn't really need any. Mother never questioned my having been at rehearsal. We'd sit through dinner talking about nothing—the play, her PTA or most recent cause or political group. Every now and then, usually in recalling some past incident, she'd mention Father by accident, pause for a second and then race on. There was something about her that was pushing itself on my attention but I kept turning it off. Her problems were hers, and mine were mine.

In the meantime I was losing weight, quite rapidly. Sally was the first person to say anything.

"Hey, Melissa! You're getting thin. You look great!"

Sally is about the only person I've ever known who is just as happy when good things happen to somebody else as to her. Then others noticed, one by one, even Terrible Ted.

"Wow, Mel, you're getting a shape. It's cool!"

I waited for Miss Ainslie to say something, and one evening, after rehearsal, she did. There were only Miss Ainslie and I left, plus a few stage assistants running around the back.

"Whatever it is you're doing, Melissa, it's working. You look very shapely. Your eyes seem much larger. And the bones in your face are beginning to show. Interesting hollows—" she touched them briefly under either cheekbone with one finger—"very good for stage appearance." She gave something that was almost a grin.

Something inside me loosened and opened up. I didn't even think about what I was going to say next. It just tumbled out. "There are a couple of things I want to ask you, Miss Ainslie, about my speech, and I know it's late. Could I walk home with you? It's on my way."

I just made that up. I hadn't an idea where she lived. It could just as easily have been across the other side of town. Also I didn't know whether she walked or drove.

"All right, Melissa. But won't your parents be worried? Aren't you expected home soon?"

"Oh, no. We never have dinner until much later. And they're out, anyway." It was only half a lie. Father certainly was out. I closed my mind to any thought of Mother.

We walked. It turned out Miss Ainslie was very pro-walk and anti-car, "that is, except for long journeys. At the rate everybody is riding, we'll be born without legs. Besides, it's excellent exercise."

I did have some questions about my speech, which seemed nothing but an excuse for the messenger to recite all the gory tragedy of the play including the suicides of both Antigone and her lover Haemon (Ted). "I mean," I said, "she doesn't seem to have any other purpose except to say 'Tell me what happened,' so that the audience can know all about what was going on offstage."

"Well, that was how offstage events, crucial to the play, were got over to the audience. Shakespeare used it, too." She looked down at me as we walked. "Do you feel that you're being short-changed—that your part isn't important enough?"

If anybody else had said this to me, I would have bristled and made some smart-mouth comeback, because it would have been a put-down. But with her it wasn't.

"I suppose so. I guess I shouldn't feel that way."

"It's natural. Do you like the theater?"

I had never thought about it, but I said immediately, "Yes!"

"How many plays have you seen?"

"Well, not too many. But I want to see more. I think —I think I want to be an actress." Such a thing had never occurred to me until that minute. But now it seemed absolutely true, as though it had always been true.

"That's a rather sudden decision," Miss Ainslie said. "Particularly since it springs from a part that you feel is nothing but a cue for somebody else's much longer speech."

"You mean, if I really wanted to act I wouldn't care how small or—or unimportant—the part."

"Ideally, I suppose. But since the vanity of all actors is notorious—and I'm just as guilty as anyone else—I can't fault you too much. But you should see how much you can put into the part, or perhaps I mean bring out of it; how much, those few minutes you're on stage, you can make Eurydice into a person, not just a cue; how much she moves the play on."

We walked for a few minutes in silence.

"All right. I'll try."

"Good girl. I think you will. To make it easier I'll tell you something about the three plays of Sophocles of which this is one—and what they're all about."

"You mean what you said before: pride and cause and effect and hubris."

"Yes, and other things. Are you interested?"

"Yes," I breathed enthusiastically.

If anyone had told me that I would voluntarily take what felt like a ten-mile walk listening to a discourse on three moldy old Greek plays and being absolutely fascinated, I would have accused them of being on something. But she talked and I listened, and then I talked about what she said, and she listened. And after a bit it stopped being about the Greek plays and went on to acting and some of her own experiences in the theater.

And then suddenly she stopped and said, "Melissa, this is where I live. Did we pass your house? You said it was on the way."

It wasn't. My house was in the exact opposite direction from school. But I waved an arm. "Oh, yes. It's back there."

It was dark by now, but there was a street lamp near where we were and she looked down into my face. "That's not true, Melissa, is it?"

It's funny about lies. Sometimes they roll off my tongue, especially to my parents. But right now it just wouldn't come. I shook my head.

"But you foolish child. Why did you walk all the way here when you're going to have to walk all the way back and then some?"

There was a silence. I cleared my throat. "I—er— wanted to talk about the play."

"In a pig's eye you did!" She looked down at me some more. "Come in, Melissa, and we'll call your mother. No, don't argue with me. I'm not going to be responsible for your walking back across town at this hour or having your parents wonder where you are."

Miss Ainslie lived in one of the new one-story apartments on the north side of town. They're like little houses, all on one floor, and have individual gardens.

She opened the front door into the living room. My first impression was that it looked comfortable and bright in a hodgepodge sort of way. Things, furniture, seemed to be of different colors, not matching at all, yet they looked well together. My next impression, galloping towards me, turned out to be a huge black Labrador who went "Whumpff" at me, then jumped up on Miss Ainslie and tried to lick her face.

"All right, all right, Nickie, yes, that's fine. I love you, too. DOWN!"

By this time I had noticed some more inhabitants. Lower jaw thrust out, a very young English bulldog waddled up and then sat on his haunches and stared at me. An enormous gray and black tiger cat, draped regally on the sofa, watched me out of lake green eyes. And, oblivious to the commotion, a very small tortoise-shell cat was carrying a kitten by the scruff of its neck across the room.

"She changes the nursery every day," Miss Ainslie said, taking off her coat. "I think she thinks she's confusing us. Well, now you know my secret vice. This black monster is Nickie. The bulldog is Hercules, the tiger over there is Tiger—very unoriginal but you run out after a while— and this is Little Mother, she was pregnant when I found her."

I didn't know which to go to first. While I was trying to choose, Nickie reared himself on his hind legs, put his paws on my shoulders and started licking my cheeks. "Oh," I gasped. It was very wet and doggy, but I was terribly pleased.

"DOWN!" Miss Ainslie said again, then she came over and hauled him down. "Now sit!" He did, but impatiently.

"Whimpf!" I looked down. The bulldog was trying to get my attention. He sneezed and I got a wet spray. He was so ugly, yet terribly appealing and somehow forlorn. I knelt down. "Hercules," I said, and rubbed him between the ears and then down his back. The effect was electric. His whole backside gyrated while he frantically tried to lick my face.

Miss Ainslie was watching with some amusement. "Despite that ferocious look he's really a marshmallow. All he wants is love, love, love. I think it's the result of too many foster homes. His present owner went to live in England and of course didn't want to put him in some kennel for six months' quarantine, which is the law there, particularly since he's still really a puppy—only eight months."

I could see what Miss Ainslie meant by love, love, love. "Whoa, Hercules," I said, trying to get my face out of reach. But I continued to stroke and pat him so he wouldn't feel rejected. "I've always wanted a dog," I said, sitting down on the floor beside him.

"Don't your parents want you to have one?"

"Well—it's just that Mother's always wanted a poodle, and Father doesn't consider that a dog at all. And nothing ever got beyond that."

"Umm. Now do you want me to call your mother, or will you?"

I looked up at her. "Do we really have to?"

"Melissa! Don't you have any consideration for her at all? She might be—probably is—worried."

"All right."

"Well, which shall it be—you or me?"

Reluctantly I got to my feet. "Where's your phone?"

"Through that door there, in the bedroom."

The bedroom was green and yellow, New England rag carpets, yellow bedspread, green curtains, watercolors on the soft green walls. Beside the telephone was a photograph, and I looked at it while I listened to the telephone ring at home. There were really three photographs, the big one in the middle and two snapshots, all of the same girl: one when she was a baby, one when she was about ten, and one when she looked about my age.

"Hello," Mother said.

"It's me, Melissa. I'm at Miss Ainslie's. We're going over my part. Don't wait dinner. I'll be home later."

"All right." She sounded funny.

"Are you all right, Mother?"

But she had hung up.

I went back into the living room. Miss Ainslie was sitting in an old wing armchair. Tiger was on her lap and Nickie was trying to be. She pushed him down. "You're not a lapdog, Nickie."

"It's okay, I told Mother."

"I know. I heard you. You have a very carrying voice, Melissa, which will be useful if you ever do decide to go on the stage. That was a modified explanation, wasn't it?"

"It wasn't exactly a lie. I mean, I *am* here, and we *were* going over my part . . ." I encountered that level gaze, "sort of."

"It fulfilled the letter. I'm not sure about the spirit. Don't you—Never mind. That's really none of my business. Off—both of you!" She picked Tiger up and put him on the floor, removed Nickie's head and shoulders from her lap and got up. "I'll drive you home."

I didn't want to leave.

"Couldn't we . . . well, just go over my speech? I mean, to make Eurydice a real person, the way you said?"

"No, not tonight. It's better for you to practice it yourself. What comes out when you play the role should come from you—not me."

"Yes, but—"

"No. Come along, Melissa, the car's down the hill in the garage."

"I thought you were anti-car," I said sullenly, following her out the front door. Hercules was making little noises of distress at being left. His ugly, unhappy face was the last thing I saw as Miss Ainslie firmly closed the door and locked it.

"Well, I am not about to send you home alone, nor do I feel at this hour like walking there and back." She sounded impatient. I mentally kicked myself all the way to the car. Here she had liked me, so Miss Eager Beaver had to go and spoil it by pushing myself on her. A great misery descended on me. We drove half the way back in silence.

I hated myself for asking, but I asked anyway. "Are you mad at me, Miss Ainslie?"

"No. But I don't like your sulking over not getting your own way. And you weren't very nice to your mother."

I wondered what Miss Ainslie would think of Mother's comment to me about my being nothing but bad luck to her. A sense of grievance that Miss Ainslie would probably call sulking filled me. When I didn't say anything, Miss Ainslie went on. "Why did you ask if she were all right, by the way? Didn't she sound it?"

I debated saying, "She sounded drunk." It could, maybe, win back her sympathy. But it would be a pretty crummy thing to do. And what was more, Miss Ainslie would be the first to think so. "She wasn't—wasn't feeling herself last night," I said, and wondered bitterly if Miss Ainslie would have thought—if she knew—that that was sacrificing the spirit for the letter of truth. Always the same —either way, I lost; heads you win, tails I lose.

We drew up to the path in front of our door. She leaned past me and pushed my door open. "Good night, Melissa. I'll see you at rehearsal tomorrow. Practice your speech."

I was barely out of the door before she drove off.

The house was dark except for the living room window. I went up to the front door and let myself in. The moment I stepped inside, a strong smell of burning rushed into my nose.

"Phew—stink," I muttered to myself, following the smell through the hall and into the kitchen. What did Mother do, forget and leave something in the oven? But it wasn't at all like her, and certainly not like Samantha, who would probably be gone by now anyway.

Like her or not, that was what had happened. And it wasn't just the oven, where a casserole of something or other had dried out and was glued to the dish. There was also a burned green mess at the bottom of a pan on the stove. Underneath it the gas, turned low, was still on, and the pan had black streaks inside and out and was sending greasy smoke up the chimney over the stove. The smell was really awful. I turned everything off. With frustration, misery and I don't know what else all pouring into a hard ball of anger somewhere in my middle, I went off to look for Mother.

I didn't have far to go, just to the living room. There, as three weeks ago, were the glass, the decanter and the bottle. And there was Mother, asleep on the sofa.

I just stood there looking at her, for how long I don't know. But at some point I registered the fact that the telephone had been ringing and then stopped.

Eight

I thought of doing a lot of things to or about Mother as I stood there, including throwing cold water on her and/or bringing her hot coffee. Miss Ainslie's statement, "You weren't very nice to your mother," changed from irony to farce. My sense of grievance mushroomed. Then I wondered if maybe Miss Ainslie was right. Maybe Mother had gotten drunk because I wasn't nice to her. Me and Father. I didn't like that thought, either. I went over to the sofa.

"Mother," I said. And then, more loudly, "Mother!"

She moaned and moved, but that was all. It was better to leave her.

I went back to the kitchen. Well, she could just clean up her own mess in the morning. But in the meantime I switched on the exhaust fan that draws the stale air up the chimney, put the pan and the casserole in the sink, filled them with water and went foraging in the refrigerator. By all the rules that ever applied to the heroines in all the romance and gothic novels I had ever read—and I devoured hundreds every year—I should have lost my appetite. I should feel a distaste at the mere thought of food. I was ravenous. The pill must have come to an abrupt end in me, or maybe I was getting immune to it or something. It occurred to me that I had better check on Mother's pill situation tonight, because I wouldn't be able to get in her room tomorrow morning.

However, I was agreeably surprised to find that after I had gobbled up half a cold chicken, I wasn't hungry any more. I glanced wistfully at the remains of a tuna fish and macaroni and cheese casserole. It looked thoroughly congealed—just the way I liked it best. There was still room in my stomach to push it in. But I thought about all the nice things people had said to me lately and shut the refrigerator door. I felt that I must be heartless to be thinking about this, worrying about my figure and weight, when Mother was passed out on the sofa. But the mere thought of Mother made me want to open the refrigerator door again. What I needed was one of Mother's sleeping pills. I was going around the kitchen making sure that everything was off when the telephone started ringing again and made me nearly jump out of my skin.

I went over and answered it. It was Miss Ainslie.

"Melissa, this is Margaret Ainslie. After I got home I started thinking I was needlessly abrupt with you and probably unfair. I realize now why, but it has nothing to do with you, that's what I wanted to make sure you understood. It's something out—something from my own life. I'm sorry."

Yesterday, having her telephone me would have been pure delight. But now it couldn't reach me across my own guilt and resentment and that prone figure in the other room that I couldn't possibly tell her about. *You weren't very nice to your mother.* No matter what she said about it not being me, I wasn't going to give her further reason to put me down and make me feel it was all my fault. Firmly I sat on the stillborn thought that in phoning she was being generous.

"It's okay, Miss Ainslie," I said.

There was a second's pause. Then, "Is your mother all right? You said she hadn't been well."

"Yes, thank you, she's fine." This time the lie rolled off with ease.

"Good night, then."

"Good night."

I went upstairs to check on the pill situation. There were plenty of diet pills left, and I helped myself to half a dozen of those, but there was only one sleeping pill. I looked at it. If she knew she just had one and found it missing, I would indeed be in the soup. On the other hand, she might not, and given the fact that she was obviously having no trouble sleeping—at least not at the moment—my need was greater than hers. I took it.

I was opening my window just before getting into bed when a blast of cold air came in. I thought about Mother on the sofa. There was no point in letting her get pneumonia. Going downstairs, I pulled a rug out from the hall closet and draped it over her. I turned out the living room light, and then decided she might fall over something, so I left a lamp on. Then I went back upstairs, took my pill and went to sleep.

Mother was up when I went down the next morning and there was no sign of the pan and the casserole dish I had left in the sink. She looked pretty bad. Her face was puffy and flushed and there was about a quarter of an inch of gray-brown hair showing at her part and hairline. I thought of the gray streaks in Miss Ainslie's and how in some way they seemed to suit her. But I put that thought away quickly. There was now another locked drawer in my mind labeled "Miss Ainslie" along with the ones labeled "Mother" and "Father" and "Ted."

Sometime in the course of the night I must have come, unconsciously, to a decision. Because it was there when I woke up. I didn't really need any of them. They were all doing their thing, whatever it was—Father living with Miss Pierce and not calling or anything, Mother getting drunk, and Miss Ainslie, like any dim adult, thinking I was sulky and not nice to Mother. So I would do mine: getting thin and being so good in my mini-part in the play that it would be thought of as one of those—what did they call them?— cameo parts.

Mother was having a bad time getting the coffee cup to her mouth. Finally she made it and swallowed some of the hot coffee. Then she managed to set the cup down.

"Thank you, Melissa, for putting the rug on me. I didn't really need it, of course, because I must have waked from my nap soon after you went to bed. Running this household alone has been extremely tiring, and having you stay out till heaven knows when doesn't help. That's why I drifted off, I suppose. Of course, I did take a drink—well, actually, two. But I'm so sensitive to alcohol that it makes me drowsy right away. Anyway, please let me know in future when you're not coming home till late, and I'll get my own dinner. That's the least you can do."

I thought about the empty decanter and half-empty bottle. That was some two drinks. But I didn't want any hassle. If I were going to make it on my own, then things would have to go smoothly.

"There's just one thing, Mother. I wish you wouldn't smoke when you drink. I don't want the house or me or you to burn down."

"I don't—" She caught my eye. "Well, sometimes when I'm unusually nervous, which, since your father went away, I have certainly had reason to be, I may take a cigarette or so."

"You had about fifteen. I counted the butts."

"I will not have you sitting in judgment over me. Do you hear me, Melissa?"

It was the same thing Father had said.

"Okay. Have it your way."

I pushed my grapefruit away, got up and started out of the kitchen.

"Melissa—"

"Yes, Mother."

She looked across the table at me. "I'm sorry."

It was funny. She looked so much older than the post-teen-ager she usually appears to be. But she also looked terribly young, almost like a child, sort of like a young, tired owl. "It's okay, Mom. Are you going to be all right?"

But she was back to her usual self. "Of course I'm going to be all right. And I want you in no later than ten, do you understand, Melissa?"

"Yes, all right."

In the days that followed I always came straight home after rehearsal. I kept seeing the stove, or a lighted cigarette rolling on the carpet. Actually, I didn't find Mother passed out again, and the liquor was always put away. But three times when I came downstairs in the morning before Mother was up, the liquor was out in the living room, so I decided she must be doing her drinking after I went to bed. Also, in the evenings, before she started drinking, there was something funny about her, not with it, unfocused.

I had taken a personal internal vow that I would not, under any circumstances, mention Father, though there were times when I had to work hard not to ask Mother if she had heard from him. But I reminded myself that even if I didn't have sovereign rights over anything else, I did over my own head, which was my kingdom, and that I had banished Father from my kingdom forever. He was the Enemy. This worked except at night when I dreamed about him. I could never remember exactly what the dreams were about, but he was in them. It was like living another life when I went to sleep, but all I could remember the next day were colors and feelings and shadows and glimpses so quick I couldn't hold onto and remember them.

I stayed clear of any you-and-me contact with Miss Ainslie, but I really studied the play and my part and for good measure I read the two preceding plays in the trilogy so I could understand it better.

One afternoon, after I had acted my part and exited, Miss Ainslie started to applaud and the others joined in. It was a sweet moment. Afterward, when we were leaving, Miss Ainslie called me over.

"Melissa, you're making Eurydice very real. Do you see now what I mean by a small part?"

"Yes. I do." Her spell was working on me, but I was determined not to give in to it.

"And you have lost a lot of weight, Melissa. You've done it very fast. Are you sure you're eating enough?"

"Oh, yes," I said gaily, almost wildly, and ran to join the others before I succumbed to her magic.

I had lately upped my diet pill to two, one in the morning and one just before rehearsal, to alleviate the ravenous hunger that descended on me when I walked through the front door at home. There was something about being at home alone with Mother every night that made me want to eat and eat and eat. Also I had finally gotten my own supply of pills by the fairly simple device of calling the drugstore, pretending I was Mother and saying that my daughter would pick them up. Then I hopped on the bus one Saturday and took the forty-five-minute ride to the next town. To buy them I had to delve into my savings, but I figured it could not be in a better cause.

Sometimes—well, often—when I wasn't on guard, I wondered why Father hadn't written to me, especially as it was going to be my sixteenth birthday on the tenth of November. And sometimes, before I could stop it, I would see him and Miss Pierce—who was looking more and more like Miss Ainslie—sitting in a green and yellow room with the lamps lit and a roaring fire and buttered toast. Why buttered toast I don't really know, except that it was cozy and warm and made me think of some of my favorite English books where everything and everybody had a place, where the curtains were always drawn and the kettle was just on the boil. Then, in my fantasy, Father would reach over and put his arms around her and kiss her, but at that point I would turn the whole thing off fast. After all, he was banished, and anyway, what did it all have to do with me?

The trouble was, the more I turned off these scenes in my mind, the more they came back and the longer they stayed. It got so that if I didn't summon all my will power and stamp on them right at the beginning, then they would become whole fantasies and they'd just take over, in class, at home, anywhere—even during the rehearsal. I wasn't getting my homework done, and while Mother never asked me about my grades these days and Father, who always did, wasn't there, I knew that sooner or later the reckoning would arrive. It was just a matter of time.

Although I didn't want to admit it to myself, I also knew that the pills were behind this. After the sleeping pill or pills—sometimes I now took two—and the dreams, I woke up dragged out and depressed. The diet pills would yank me out of that into a sort of euphoria and then I'd fight off the temptation to fantasize. But I couldn't bear to stop taking them. I had lost eighteen pounds and I looked—especially in the new jeans and sweaters I had bought—absolutely sensational. My face, instead of being round, was triangular, with wide forehead and cheekbones and pointed chin. My eyes did look large. And my hair was longer and swingier. I had become svelte, sightly and shapely and I reveled in it.

The strange part was that although now I had my heart's desire and several of the most attractive boys asked me out, I didn't go. It isn't that I didn't want to, at least I don't think so. But for one thing, there were nightly rehearsals; for another, I was scared of anybody coming to the house, not knowing how Mother would be. She might be drinking, or she might be on one of the queer jags that had taken her lately when she talked nonstop without making too much sense. These weird talkathons had been occurring at dinner or over the weekend. They irritated me a lot at first because I assumed I was supposed to make some kind of appropriate reply, and the way she skipped from subject to subject there was nothing I could get hold of to reply to. But after a few half-hearted efforts, I realized that it was a one-man—or rather one-woman—show. Replies were not expected, so I just relaxed and let her run on. Mother has always had a tendency to run on unless stopped forcibly because the party or whatever was over, or by Father's ability to collect the topic together and close it in one incisive comment. But I guess Father's absence had really pulled the plug out.

This didn't happen all the time. Occasionally we'd bat a little conversation back and forth.

"What did you do, today, Melissa?"

"Oh, nothing much. The usual. School, classes." I'd hurry past that in case she suddenly took it into her head to ask about my grades. "And we had a really good rehearsal last night. Joel is getting to be a sensational actor."

"That's nice." And then, after a minute, "Do I know Joel?" Which was a real change and should have alerted me that something was very wrong with Mother. In the old days she practically had an FBI dossier on every eligible boy at school. But I was so bent on not making the smallest wave that I would tell her in a general way who Joel was and then ask, "And what did you do today, Mother?"

"Like you, the usual. Had my hair done, went to the PTA meeting. Talked to the carpenter about those shelves upstairs that need fixing."

There was nothing very unusual about those exchanges except that they weren't real. As the commercials say, they were buffered, on both sides, because neither of us wanted to talk about anything that was really happening.

And then everything blew up.

I'm still not sure I understand why it happened, although the doctor explained to me afterward about cumulative effect. I didn't do anything different from any other day, except take my second diet pill a little earlier than usual, because the last class had been canceled so that we could have longer rehearsal time. Dress rehearsal would be in another three weeks, and we weren't ready. As Miss Ainslie explained it to us, although *Antigone* was neither long nor complicated, it required all the better acting for having so little activity; everything depended on *what* we said and *how* we said it, not on a whole lot of characters rushing on and offstage. And she finished it off by saying that up until now she had never been in or directed a second-rate performance of any play, and she wasn't about to begin.

So the cast and chorus collected in the auditorium and I gulped down my pill on the way, figuring it could take the place of lunch.

Joel caught up with me as we were walking over. "Still mad at me?"

The answer to that was yes, though I couldn't recall at the moment what I was mad about. Then I remembered. "You mean your crack about 'Anything for a little popularity'?"

"I shouldn't have said it, and anyway, I'm as bad as you are."

"I hadn't noticed you putting yourself out to win friends and influence people."

"No. That's the point. I'm trying not to. It's known as overcompensation."

"Joel, I have a hard time believing that. You're such a—a loner. Not a crowd person at all. I mean, you really do your own thing—whatever it is."

"But then you haven't known me very long, have you?"

As a matter of fact, I hadn't. None of us had. He'd arrived in the middle of the term last year and until the play had walked by himself.

I looked at him. "What's there to tell, Joel?"

He looked straight at me and said, "Maybe sometime I'll tell you."

Something different about Joel's appearance had been nagging at my attention. When he looked straight at me I knew what it was.

"Joel, you don't have on your glasses! You look super! You have really great eyes!" And he did. They were long, with black lashes, and were a light clear gray that really dressed up his face and made it interesting.

Joel's thin cheeks reddened. "Thanks," he said gruffly.

"I got some contact lenses. You look pretty cool yourself. In fact—"

But by this time we were at the door of the auditorium squashing in with several dozen other kids.

Joel put out his hand quickly and took mine. "Can I talk to you later?"

"Sure, of course." I was surprised to feel as excited as I did over old Joel. In fact, I was feeling fluttery and soaring, both. I should have had lunch, I thought. Some of it was undoubtedly Joel, but not all.

As the rehearsal wore on I felt stranger and stranger. The nearest way I can describe it is that everything was happening an octave higher, but nothing seemed to connect. I was having a hard time judging what was going on. Everything appeared unrelated to everything else and some of it was wildly funny, only apparently nobody but me thought so. Joel was up on the stage practically all the time, but at a break he came down and sat beside me. We didn't talk much. I was jumpy and nervous and had a hard time sitting still and was given to breaking suddenly into noisy giggles.

"Are you okay, Melissa? You look funny."

"Thanks," I said and giggled. "I thought you said I looked cool," and I giggled again. It was hilariously funny, and I couldn't understand why he didn't see it.

"Can we have some quiet back there," Miss Ainslie called, coming to the edge of the stage. "Melissa, please keep your voice down. It's not like you to interrupt a rehearsal. Joel, come back up here."

Joel stood up, but he bent down towards me. "Are you on something, Mel?" he asked urgently, and took hold of my arm so hard it hurt.

"Let go of me," I shouted.

There was a burst of laughter from the auditorium and even on the stage.

"Unhand me, sir," somebody squeaked.

"Poor old Joel, what a time to try and make out."

I could see Joel's face. His eyes, now visible without the glasses and very expressive, had a sort of funny blaze in them. Then he whirled around and walked down the aisle towards the stage.

The next hour—at least I think it was an hour—was a nightmare. By this time I wasn't just giggly and strange and high, I was feeling as though I had absolutely no control over anything I did. Wild colors were swirling around inside and outside my head. I had lost my ability to judge sound—whether it was soft or loud—and any sense of whether something was appropriate or not. If I ever got up on the stage I knew I couldn't hang on. I would freak out entirely.

I didn't know what to do. I had not meant to embarrass Joel. It just happened. Sally and Ann were up on the stage so I couldn't speak to either one. If I made any more interruptions I might be thrown out of the play. A couple of the chorus kids who had tried it on once too often had been, and Miss Ainslie had said at the time "And that goes for everyone else in the cast, including the leads, right up to the night of the performance. I'd rather scratch a play than have anyone threaten it or the rest of you or me with destructive and unprofessional behavior. Capish?"

We all got it.

I wasn't even sure I could make it out of the auditorium without blowing up or something. I was really scared.

But I started across the back. Luckily, everyone was watching the stage.

I had got through the auditorium door and into the lobby and was clinging to the wall, which seemed to be tipping, when Joel came out.

"All right, Mel. I'm taking you to the school nurse."

That was exactly what I wanted to avoid. "No, Joel, please. I'll be all right. At least, maybe you could help me get home."

"I'm not helping you anywhere unless you tell me what you've been on. And don't say, nothing. I know about drugs. Have you been taking speed, amphetamines?"

"Of course not."

"Then what is it? I bet you even have some on you, because you sure weren't like this this morning, but I've been watching you lately, and I was beginning to think you are tripping on something. Mel, you idiot—"

Now I was crying. "It's not true, Joel. You have no right to say that."

"Yes, I do. Show them to me."

"Joel, no—"

"Come on, or I'll look for them myself."

I didn't want to fight, I guess. I reached into my pocket and pulled out the folded tissue. I had two diet pills (I always kept an extra supply in my jeans in case I left in a hurry and forgot) and, by accident, one sleeping pill.

Joel picked up the orange and blue diet pill. "Speed. Just as I thought. And a sleeping pill. Why did you lie, as if I didn't know?"

"They're *diet* pills, Joel. Mother has them."

"Diet pills are speed. They have amphetamine in them,

like a bennie or a dexie or any of that crowd. Oh, Mel, I wish I'd told you—"

"Told me what?"

"What I was going to tell you before. My older sister got hooked on these. I don't even know where she is now. She was sixteen. And I got into them a little—not much. Just because I didn't want to be an oddball. I was lucky, I had a bad trip almost right away. That's why I came across the country to live with Dad. I'd rather be dead than take these, Mel, I've seen what they do. Come on, I'm taking you to the nurse."

"Please don't, Joel. Please. They'll tell Mother and take me out of the play. I didn't know they were speed. I just wanted to get thin. You know how kids made fun of me when I was fat. Nobody even looked at me. Even Father—" At that, when I thought about Father, the whole house came down. I couldn't stop crying.

I realized Joel was taking me somewhere and finally I saw that we were in one of the little coat rooms off the lobby. Joel pushed me on a sort of bench and closed the door. Then he sat down beside me, put his arm around me and told me to cry it out.

I did. I cried and cried, and in between I told him about Father and Mother and what had happened at home. By the time I finished I was feeling a little better. Less like I were on the flying trapeze.

"Cripes, Mel, why didn't you tell me? I know how you feel. My parents separated. Mother's out in Colorado and Dad's here. Dad's a drunk, an alcoholic, but still I like him better. You remember when one of those cops spoke to me you said it sounded like they knew me? Well, they do.

Every now and then I have to go down to the station house and get Father."

"Oh, Joel." I took his hand. His arm was still around me. I looked at him. He looked at me. Then he kissed me. It was a funny moment for such a spectacular event. It was warm and sweet and wonderful. I hadn't even imagined how nice it would be. And when I had imagined it, it had been with Ted. Now the mere thought of him turned me off. I put my free arm on Joel's shoulder and we kissed again.

It was at that moment that the door opened and Miss Ainslie walked in.

"If you want to hide, you shouldn't make so much noise."

Nine

The next few minutes were pretty hairy. Miss Ainslie was angry. And fluent, witty and biting. "Not that I have the faintest interest in what you do in your spare time, nor the slightest desire to censor or inhibit your amusement, whatever it is. But this is not your spare time. It is rehearsal time, of which we do not have the beginning of enough. Our only ghost of a chance of putting on a creditable performance a month from now is to think about little else between now and then. Joel—do you realize that we have been waiting for you for the last fifteen minutes? I gave the cast a ten-minute break—not the night off. If you don't want the part, say so. I'll find someone else or call off the performance."

Joel had risen. "Look, Miss Ainslie—"

She ploughed straight over him. "And as for you, Melissa, with your childish performance in the audience today, I shouldn't be surprised—"

"Now, just a minute," Joel snapped. "Melissa's—er—not well. She-she—"

I realized that Joel was trying to excuse me without giving me away and was making Miss Ainslie madder by the minute. He'd lose the part. I got up.

"It's my fault, Miss Ainslie," I quaked out. "I've been taking diet pills. I didn't know that they'd—well, flip me out the way they did. I just wanted to get thin. I didn't know they're what everybody calls 'speed.' But it's not Joel's fault. He was bawling me out. He said—" I was about to mention his sister and his own experience when I remembered that of course I couldn't. I had to finish it, so I said reluctantly, "He said I had to go to the nurse, but I was trying to get out of it."

There was a pause.

"I suppose I should blame myself," Miss Ainslie said. "It occurred to me once or twice that you might be, and you were losing so quickly. I should have asked you and made you tell me the truth. Do you realize people can lose their minds with speed? Die?"

"I do now. I didn't really connect . . ." I was about to say, Mother's diet pill, but that didn't sound right.

"Where did you get them?" Miss Ainslie asked.

"I stole them. From Mother," I said finally.

"Does your mother know you're taking them?"

I shook my head.

"Then she must be informed."

"Miss Ainslie—please don't." I could just see everything coming out. Father's leaving, Mother's drinking. I also realized something else: that I was very tired of holding it all alone. Now I had Joel who would help me. But I still didn't want a big public display, even though that meant I must have terribly middle-class values.

"But your mother has to know, Melissa. You must realize that. Either that or I tell the principal, who will tell your mother."

Joel said, "She's got to, Mel."

"But you know about Mother, I told you."

"Maybe this will help her get back on the road."

"What's the matter with your mother, Melissa?" Miss Ainslie asked.

"She drinks."

"Well, what about your father?"

"He's left. For good."

Joel took my hand and glared defiantly at Miss Ainslie.

She said, "I see. I'm sorry. I'm also remembering that night when you were at my apartment. If I hadn't been taken up with my own memories I could have been more help to you." She paused. "You see, Melissa, I had a daughter. It's a long story, but suffice it to say I wasn't much of a mother. I was always going to be, but something else always seemed to be more important. All I could think of when I heard you speak to your mother was that at least she was there, and that you didn't appreciate that. In other words, I wasn't listening to you or thinking about you, I was thinking about myself."

I didn't know what to say. I was remembering the picture of the girl in Miss Ainslie's bedroom and wondering what had happened to her.

She took a breath. "Look, would it help if I talked to your mother?"

"You mean after you've told her about my taking diet pills?"

"Yes. Or would you rather I talked to your father about it?"

"No."

"He's still your father, even though he isn't at home."

"He doesn't care about me."

"Are you sure that's true? Do you really believe it?"

I stared down at my toes. I knew in another minute I would cry again.

Finally I said, "I don't know what I believe."

"All right. Joel, you'd better take her home. I'll rehearse the others around you both the rest of the time. Melissa—it's a rule of the school that when any of our students is found taking drugs, for whatever reason, someone from the school has to inform at least one parent. Since you seem to have stumbled into this without meaning to, and you don't look as if you've enjoyed it, I'm willing to let Joel take you home instead of to the nurse's or principal's office. Decide who should be told. If I don't get a call from either your mother or your father by tomorrow afternoon, then I'll have to report it to the principal and let him take it from there. And if I ever hear of your taking one of those poisonous pills again, or suspect that you are, you'll be in real trouble."

"All right. I knew I shouldn't. But I'll get fat, and I would rather die."

"You don't have to get fat. A close friend of mine is

one of the best nutritionists in the state. I'll drive you over to see her Saturday. Okay?"

"Yes. Thanks." My gloom lifted a little. "Do you really think she'll be able to keep me thin?"

"She can give you all kinds of information, encouragement, help—incidentally, she is—or was—a fellow sufferer. Nobody can *do* it but you. Certainly not those diabolical pills. Did you find they were as effective later as when you began?"

"No. I started taking two. Maybe that's why I flipped out this afternoon. I took the second one too soon and with no lunch."

"You were lucky it wasn't worse. Do I have your word of honor you won't touch one again?"

It was a wrench. They had made not eating so easy. But I was good and scared. "Yes. I promise."

"And you will tell your mother—or your father?"

"Yes."

"All right. I expect to hear from one or the other."

She surprised me then by leaning down and kissing my cheek. "Don't risk losing yourself, Melissa. You have so much."

Joel walked me home. When we entered the house we found Mother with the television on and the decanter and glass beside her. It was, of course, earlier than I usually came home.

"Hello, Mother," I said, walking in. "This is Joel Martin."

Mother looked annoyed. "You're home early."

I took a deep breath. If I waited till later my courage might fail altogether. Besides, Joel was there and that made me feel stronger. "Mother, I got sent home from rehearsal because I—I sort of freaked out this afternoon. I've been taking pills, diet pills, and sleeping ones. Yours. Miss Ainslie said I had to tell you or—or Father. And she wants you to call her tonight or tomorrow so she can discuss the matter with you. It's a school rule."

"I *thought* some of my pills were missing. I didn't realize you'd *steal*. I really can't understand, Melissa, with all I've had to put up with lately, why you have to go and do something like that. All you had to do was tell me you wanted to take a diet pill and I would have got a much milder one for you. Of course you were terribly overweight, and I daresay it was necessary for you to do something drastic to get all that fat off. But what the school will think when I have to call up as though I were the one who was remiss, I can't imagine."

She raised her glass, saw it was empty, and picking it up went over to the sideboard to the ice bucket. Her speech was a little slurred, not too much. She showed how much she had drunk much more in the way she walked. A sort of fury seized me.

"After all *you've* been through! I could have died or gone mad with those pills. I suppose you just think this is more of my being bad luck for you? You're the one who's been at me and at me about losing weight. It's all you ever talk about, as though it's the only thing in the world that matters."

Mother turned. "You have no right to blame me. All I

wanted was for you to be attractive. No boy would ever look at you the way you were."

"Is that the end of the world?" I shouted. I had forgotten Joel standing in the back of the room.

He spoke up. "Take it easy, Mel. It won't do any good. Not the way she is. Besides, it's never any use blaming other people. It doesn't do anything for you."

Mother swirled around. "How dare you speak of me like that? As though I were a—a—"

"A drunk? My father is. Why shouldn't you be? It's not a disgrace. That is, if you do something about it."

Then she started to cry, sitting huddled in the corner of the sofa. "It's all your father's fault," she said. "He ought to be here."

Joel looked at me. His expression said, "See what I mean?"

My anger faded. "All right, Mother. Never mind."

I went over to her and sat on the arm of the sofa and put my arm around her. It didn't seem quite natural, and I felt—nothing. Not pity, not compassion, not love, more like I was acting out something under false pretenses.

I looked across the room. "Thanks, Joel. Thanks a lot."

He went to the door and turned. "Melissa, you won't— you promised . . ."

"No. I won't. I promise."

It was not a very successful evening.

Samantha had left a casserole which I heated up, and I made a salad. I tried to get Mother to drink some coffee, but she wouldn't. Nor did she eat very much. But she brought her glass to the table.

"I wish you wouldn't drink so much, Mother."

"I don't drink that much. It's just that I'm upset."

"Why are you upset?"

"How could I not be upset, Melissa, with your father gone? That's a silly question."

I had come down off my high and was feeling flat and let down and depressed. "To listen to you, anybody would think it was some kind of hand-in-hand-in-the-sunset marriage. All you did was fight."

"That doesn't mean I didn't love him."

I put down my fork. "You're in love with Father?"

Mother turned her glass around. "What's 'in love'? It doesn't mean anything. A marriage is a marriage."

"Well, if that is what a happy marriage is, I don't think much of it."

"Who are you to judge? What do you know about love?"

"Not much. But if that's what marriage is, no wonder it's a failing institution like I read in the paper the other day. You and Father never even acted as if you liked each other or wanted to be together. And I was always in the middle. What you wanted me to do, he didn't, and what Father wanted me to do, you wouldn't want. No wonder I've never really known what I was supposed to be. I was the ball in the ball game." I stared at her and found her staring back. "And now that he's left, you're falling apart."

"Oh, leave me alone." Which was really weird; it was what I was always saying.

Mother got slowly out of her chair. "I'm tired of arguing. I'm tired of everything. I know I haven't helped much, Melissa. I know I should be doing something about you now. But I can't. Not tonight. Maybe tomorrow. But not tonight. I'm going to bed."

I heard her go upstairs. I washed the dishes and was watching a show on television when the doorbell rang.

When I opened the door, there stood Miss Ainslie. On a leash was Hercules, looking glum and pessimistic. When he saw me, though, he started wiggling his backside and making whiffling noises.

"I thought you might like to have a friend," Miss Ainslie said. "In this bag are a couple of cans of dog food."

Hercules and I were having an emotional reunion. "Please come in. How long can I keep him?"

"All his life, I hope. He needs a permanent home. And as I told you, all he's interested in is love and more love."

We went into the living room. "Are you sure? I'd love to have him."

"Quite sure. As you know, I have more than enough wildlife, and Nickie and Tiger are my special long-term animals. The others are merely there until I can force them on somebody."

"How can I thank you? I've always wanted a dog!"

"You have. Is your mother here?"

"She's in bed, Miss Ainslie. I did tell her, truly. Ask Joel."

"I believe you. And I didn't come to check up on you. I really did come to bring you Hercules. But I was thinking about your family situation and wondering if I could do anything to help."

I shook my head. "I can't think of anything."

"Where *is* your father? Is he far?"

"No. In New York."

"Has he been in touch with you?"

"No. And Mother hasn't said anything about his calling while I was at school."

"You're very angry at him, aren't you, Melissa?"

"Yes."

"Why don't you at least try to get in touch with him?"

"I told you. He doesn't really like me. Mother told me—" I realized I was telling Miss Ainslie something Mother wouldn't want her to know, but I didn't care. "Mother told me that they had to get married. I mean, she was pregnant with me. And he didn't really want to. And I think he's resented me ever since."

"But you've never talked to him about it."

"No. I'm not going to go around begging him to love me."

"No. You certainly shouldn't do that. But remember, you've only heard this from one side. I'm not saying your mother falsified anything. But before you judge him altogether, why don't you at least hear his side? You don't even know his side about leaving home."

"Mother said it was my fault. I suggested it. And I did. We had a flaming row and I told him to go and live with— well, somebody he's supposed to be interested in. Then I ran out for the evening and went to a double-feature movie. When I got back he was gone. And that was the first time I ever saw Mother drunk, even though I knew she liked to drink."

"Well, you don't really know that there isn't more to it than that. I think you ought to give him at least a chance to talk to you."

"I've been here. He knew where to find me. I didn't run away."

"You don't know all the circumstances, Melissa. Maybe he thinks you don't love him. Did you ever think of that?"

She got up. "I don't want to overpersuade you to do anything you really don't want to do. But think it over."

We started towards the door. "What happened to your daughter?" I asked. It had been bothering me.

"Oh—a lot of things, some of them not so good, some of them very good, like finding something she really liked to do and getting married to the man she wanted and having a couple of children she seems to enjoy thoroughly."

"Do you get on? I mean, now?"

"Yes. But two things had to happen for that to come about. I had to acknowledge that I was wrong about a lot of things; that was the easy part because it was so obvious. And she had to step over her resentment and fear of me—you've seen my temper; believe me, it used to be much worse!— and tell me how she felt. That was the part that took guts. At least then we had something we could work with."

"I didn't even know you'd been married—I mean, being called 'Miss Ainslie.' "

She grinned. "My married name was Hochstedther. You can see why I kept my maiden name for the stage. And after the divorce, it was silly to use anything else."

Hercules and I saw her to the door. I thought for a minute he was going to follow her out. But he didn't. He stopped at the threshold and stood there, panting gently.

"I hope your mother doesn't mind about Hercules," she said.

"She won't. Besides, he's mine. And I'll look after him."

She stooped down. " 'Bye, Hercules. I think you're going to have a long, coddled and happy life."

Ten

I expected to sleep the sleep of the saved and wake up full of resolve and power, ready to tackle the problem of Father.

It didn't work out that way.

For one thing, my bed is fairly narrow, and Hercules liked the middle of it. If I put him at the foot or in the carton beside the bed that I'd lined with a blanket and one of my sweaters, he cried. So we compromised; that is, he kept the middle of the bed and I learned to lie around him. But it wouldn't have made much difference anyway. I couldn't sleep. I thought I felt so tired and drained I'd just pop off, in spite of the fact that I had been taking two sleeping pills regularly.

It didn't work out that way, either.

After an hour or two of trying to get to sleep I was ready to climb the walls. I knew some more sleeping pills were no farther than my secret desk drawer. I was so scared I'd succumb that I finally got up and emptied them down the john, along with the rest of the diet pills. Then I went back to bed and tried again to go to sleep. Then I read for a while; then I watched the late, late science fiction show on my mini-television set. Then I watched the horror movie after that. Then I finally went to sleep. An hour and a half later my alarm went off. I felt terrible.

Mother wasn't down at breakfast, but I left a letter explaining about Hercules, and a note for Samantha who would be in that day. She loves animals.

For about four days I felt utterly crummy, physically and mentally. Everything seemed flat and pointless. I had no energy and I had trouble sleeping at night. If it hadn't been for Hercules and Joel, not necessarily in that order, I don't know whether I could have stuck it. Mother and I said almost nothing to each other. She was never up when I left, and while she wasn't passed out or anything when I came home, I was pretty sure she had been drinking steadily and it seemed now to make her morose and silent.

I was worried about her reaction to Hercules and how he fared after his first day. He met me at the door when I got home, and after we had had our greeting, we went back to the kitchen. Mother was fixing dinner. A glass half full of what looked like bourbon was on the kitchen table.

After a few meaningless exchanges about her day and mine I said, "How do you like Hercules?"

Mother stared at him for a long moment. "He looks like Winston Churchill."

"Is that good? I mean, did you admire him?"

"I suppose so. I'm a Francophile and prefer poodles. Perfidious Albion and all that. But he's your dog, not mine, and as you said in your note, you'll take care of him."

Later that evening I caught her slipping Hercules some pot roast from her plate and decided not to worry any more.

To cap everything else, I got summoned by the principal over my grades, which had at last caught up with me, and in the course of trying to explain about them I admitted taking pills, and everything really hit the fan.

Mr. Stacey, the principal, never actually said the word "expel." But the idea was certainly hovering in the air as he talked about my example to other kids and the fact that our school had stayed remarkably free of the drug epidemic and he intended to keep it that way. The frustrating part was, I couldn't really feel too victimized. I knew what he was saying was right; my own experience, small as it was, told me that.

But at the point where I thought I had really had it, Miss Peabody, my homeroom teacher, who had been confided in by Miss Ainslie, came in and spoke up for me. And shortly after that Miss Ainslie herself showed up and did the same.

I got let off with a long talking-to and a bad scare and an order to go and see Dr. Hastings, or else.

So I went to see Dr. Hastings. He listened to everything I had to say, and I waited for the bricks to fall on my head. Instead he said, "How do you feel?"

There was something in his voice that made me think he might not be the old dodo I'd thought. "Rotten," I said.

"Specifically?"

So I told him specifically.

He got up and came back with a syringe. "I'm going to give you a high-powered vitamin shot. That should make you feel better. In another day or so you'll feel back to normal."

Then he gave me a long talk on the subject of nutrition and weight and diet and handed me a couple of books to read.

"Now," he said. "It's up to you."

I glanced at the books. "Won't I ever be able just to relax and eat what I want?"

"Probably not. But it needn't be a perpetual Lent. You just have to make up your mind what you want most for yourself and stick to it. You can make it interesting, or you can make it a penance."

I sighed. "Okay, I'll try." Then I remembered about Miss Ainslie's friend, the nutritionist, and told the doctor about her.

"That's good. I think I know who she is and she's excellent."

I stood up. "Thanks."

"Not so fast. Now tell me about your mother. Is she drinking?"

"How did you know? Did she call you?"

"Not hardly. But word gets around. When is your father coming home?"

"I don't think he is."

"He has a right to know what's going on. Somebody has to tell him. I'll do it if you want. But I think it would be much better if you did. What about it, Melissa?"

"All right. I guess I was meaning to, anyway."

That evening I called Joel and told him about my visit with Dr. Hastings and what I had decided to do. "I've already talked to Miss Ainslie and explained, and she'll tell Miss Peabody so I can be given an excused absence."

"Do you want me to go with you, Mel? I'll be glad to."

I would have liked very much to have him come with me, but I knew I had to go alone. "I'd love it, Joel, but I think I have to do this by myself. Would you come by as soon as school is out and give Hercules a walk?" He and Hercules had already met.

"Sure. By the way, happy birthday for tomorrow."

"Thanks. Wish me luck."

"You'll do okay. I'll talk to you when you get back. Maybe you can make it back in time for rehearsal. I—er— have something for you."

"You do? What?"

"You'll just have to wait and see. It'll be an incentive for you to hightail it back. Don't worry about Hercules."

I left early while Mother was still asleep. I'd never been to Father's office before. During the night I had thought about writing to him instead. But I knew that wouldn't do. I had to see him. And I had to see him away from home. I didn't care how many meetings or clients or anything else he had scheduled. Furthermore, although nobody except Joel seemed to have remembered, it was my birthday. I was sixteen. An adult. Almost.

And there was one more thing. I would get to see Miss Pierce. If I had called Father he might have arranged for her to be out.

I put on a new brown pants suit that made me look really tall and thin—even in that mirror that Mother had had put on my closet door—and a green shirt, and I carried a new over-the-shoulder bag. I took a bus to the station, a train to Grand Central and the subway down to Wall Street.

The double oak doors said in square gold lettering, *Carteret, Williams, FitzRoy and Hammond.* There was a very cool female sitting at the reception desk who looked in no danger of thawing when I walked in. She raised her brows. "Yes?"

I said aggressively, "I'm Melissa Hammond. I've come to see my father. Please tell him I'm here." Could she be Miss Pierce?

"Oh! I'm sorry! I didn't know you. Of course."

Miss Iceberg was melting all over the place and now looked not much older than me. She said into the phone, "Miss Pierce, Melissa Hammond is here to see her father." She put the receiver down. "Miss Pierce will be right out."

For a brief, idiotic moment, I wondered if Father would try and stuff her through the window.

There was the sound of footsteps. A woman with dark hair and eyes came in view from around a corner behind the reception desk. She wasn't at all pretty or young or what I expected, whatever that was. Yet she looked somehow all together, and she had what Mother calls style. For a second or two she looked at me with an odd, questioning expression, as though she were weighing me up. Then her eyes crinkled at the corners. She had a really good smile. "I'm glad to meet you, Melissa." And she held out her hand.

I just stared at her. Then, without thinking, I held out mine. "H-how do you d-do?"

"Your father has a client with him and I haven't interrupted him. I'll tell him you're here. I know how pleased he'll be." She paused again. I was waiting for her to take me back. Then she said rather hesitantly, "And we could have some coffee or a soda, if you like, until he's free."

Spurning the offer, sitting rigidly in the waiting room until my father deigned to see me, turning around and going back to Westchester, all flitted through my mind. I didn't do any of them. Somehow I found myself in a coffee shop in the lobby of the building, sitting in a booth across the table from the Woman in Father's Life. All I could think of was how totally unlike a mistress she looked, at least according to what I had read about mistresses. She didn't look at all like Sin, which somehow I had associated with bosoms and velvet hangings and strong, sexy perfume. Although if one wished to be logical, they wouldn't go at all well in an office.

"You know, Melissa," she said when her coffee and my diet soda had arrived, "I am really glad to meet you. Your father has talked of you so much."

I found this hard to believe and decided she was trying to con me. "Has he?"

"Yes. He has." She gave me back look for look. There was something about the square forehead and deep-set eyes that spelled intelligence, lots of it.

"I d-don't see how he could do that. I don't think he knows me very well." I was stammering nervously, but determined to be belligerent. "I guess you know him b-better."

"Perhaps I do." Cool as a cucumber.

We drank our coffee and soda in silence for a minute.

Then she said, "I know that you're feeling—hostile, but—"

"Wouldn't you?" I just blurted it out without thinking, scared and embarrassed but determined not to back down.

"That depends, doesn't it, on what I thought I had to be hostile about."

So there it lay between us. But I couldn't make myself ask her the final question: Are you Father's mistress? I could hear the words in my head, but I couldn't get them through my mouth. There was another sticky pause, then she said, "There's something I have to tell you. It's about your father. Do you think you could listen for a few minutes without—without prejudice?"

It made me feel a little better to realize she was almost as nervous as I was.

"All right," I said, deliberately ungracious, clinging to the thought of Mother left at home. "What is it?"

"Your father is shortly going to have to undergo a very serious operation on his leg. He's been in Walter Reed Hospital for the last three weeks having tests of every kind, and he has to go back there next week."

It hit like a bomb. But all I could think to say was, "He's been there for *three weeks?* Is *that* where he's been? Why didn't he tell us? Why didn't he tell me?"

She didn't answer that.

"I don't think he told Mother, either. But he told you."

"Well, he had to, because of the work here. It wasn't necessarily a personal thing."

"He never tells anybody anything. Not really. He's always being ironic or—or detached."

"It's the way he copes with situations that are unpleasant, or painful or even frightening."

"Frightening! I can't imagine him ever being frightened at anything, or admitting that anything ever hurt him."

She was stirring her coffee around and around. "But that doesn't mean he can't be hurt, physically—or in other ways. As I said, it's a mechanism with him, like crying or talking is with other people. It also doesn't mean he doesn't care—for you, for instance." She stopped stirring and looked up at me. "He loves you and worries about you and is wounded and bewildered when all he seems to evoke from you is antagonism, so he backs off. He has pride, too, you know."

"With me?"

"Don't you, with him?"

I was wondering, with Mother? But Mother was not in this conversation. Without ever mentioning her, Miss Pierce ("Pierce" certainly didn't suit her; neither, for that matter, did "Miss") had firmly put her to one side and drawn a line between Father and me. It occurred to me at that moment that there had never been a line, a line of communication, just between Father and me. Mother, in some way or other, was really in everything we ever said to one another. Was that why, when he drove me to school and tried to reach me, show me affection, I got scared and retreated? Then there were those last loving words "I hate you!" I flung at him. It felt brave and revolutionary when I said it. Now it just seemed crude and cruel and childish.

"Why are you telling me this, about his leg and the hospital? I'd get to know it anyway, wouldn't I? Or is he just going to the hospital without telling us?"

"No. Of course not. It's because I think he needs you now. I mean—I think he needs very much to feel that you love him. And I was afraid that if I didn't tell you, you might not know it, you might not read it into what he says or the way he says it or the way he acts." She smiled faintly. "As you said, he retreats into being ironic or detached."

When did Mother ever plead for Father like this? Never that I could remember. On the other hand there was my own grievance, alive and painfully kicking.

"He's never needed me before. He's never done anything but criticize me. I'm too this, too that, not enough of something else. It's hard to get a need to be loved out of that kind of feedback. He's never loved me as me. And I'm tired of having to be something else before somebody can love me."

There was another of those silences. I sucked up my soda as noisily as possible, absolutely determined not to cry.

"Melissa—my dear! Of course you don't have to be something else. If he's made you feel that—"

"Well, he has. You seem to know him so well—much better than Mother and me—why don't you ask him? If he wants me to be friends with him, why hasn't he been friends with me? Why doesn't he ever say anything nice or kind? And why does he tell *you* all this?" Pushing the glass away, I got up. "I'm going upstairs to see him." And I walked to the coffee shop door. As I waited for the elevator she came up and then the elevator opened and we got in. I was hoping somebody else would get in but we rode to the eighth floor alone. I kept my eyes on the floor. She didn't say anything till just before the elevator doors opened again. Then she said, "I'm sorry I made you angry, Melissa. Forgive me."

Father was standing by his window when I came in, his back to the gray, shining river that I could see on either side of him. He said, "Hello, Melissa. I'm glad you came to see me."

One of the things that's always been so difficult about Father, as far as I am concerned, is that he is so good-looking. It's always made me feel dwindled. And I could feel the process happening again. But suddenly I remembered Joel and felt less dwindled. I saw then that if it weren't for Joel—no matter what the doctor had said—I wouldn't be here at all. A great feeling of gratitude filled me and I determined that I would tell him as soon as I got back. Joel, with his ex-harelip, would understand.

Then Father took a step forward and I saw that his limp was much worse and that his face looked tired and drawn and tight. "Melissa?" he said nervously. *Nervously.* It looked like Miss Pierce was right.

A hard angry knot of resentment somewhere in my middle dissolved. I went up to him and said the first thing that came into my head. "Daddy, I'm sorry I said I hated you. I didn't mean it."

"I deserved it."

"And I'm sorry about your leg. Does it hurt?"

Normally Father would say "No" or "It'll be all right." In fact, he started to. And then he stopped and looked at me. "As a matter of fact, it hurts like blazes."

"I'm sorry. Truly." And I put my arms around him.

For a second he seemed astonished. Then he hugged me so hard I thought my ribs would crack.

"By the way," he said after a minute. "Happy birthday."

"You remembered!"

"Of course. It was a very important day in my life."

"Truly?"

"Truly, Melissa. I'm sorry I haven't made it plainer. I don't mean—I can't—it's difficult for me to explain. You think I don't love you, but I do. But I don't know how to let you know."

"You know, Daddy, all I really wanted was to please you and have you like me."

"Well, you do. You please me very much even though I know I haven't showed it. By the way, you look lovely, if a little on the skinny side. You must have been dieting. Are you all right?"

It was a golden moment. One of my fantasies has always been for somebody to tell me I am too skinny.

"Father, I have to tell you something about that—I mean about me losing weight. And something else, about Mother."

"All right. Come over here and sit down and talk to me."

So we sat on the sofa in his office and I told him about the pills and the play and me.

"Listen to me, Melissa. I want you to promise me that you won't touch one of those again."

"It's all right. I have promised. I don't like what they do."

"A third of the people in this country are on something—liquor, pot, pills or hard drugs. Please don't be one of them. It's not living and it's not worth it."

"That's what Joel said."

"Who is Joel?"

So I told him about Joel. "He kissed me. It was the first time anybody kissed me. Of course, most of the girls I know got kissed when they were fourteen. But—"

"Sixteen is quite early enough. May I meet him?"

"Yes." I looked up at him. "Are you coming home now?"

"I thought we might have a lunch in honor of your birthday, and then go home together."

"Super. Where?"

"At my club? Would you like that? If not, anywhere you choose."

I was thrilled. I'd never been to Father's club. "Your club is great."

"I have a present for you."

Father pulled a box out of his pocket. I opened it and saw a really stupendous watch on a long, gold chain. "Oh wow!" I took it out of the box. "It's really super, Daddy. I mean it's great. I love it. Thank you."

He put it around my neck. "It occurred to me afterward that you've always wanted a dog and you might prefer that. You may have both if you like. We can get one before you go home."

So I told him about Hercules.

"An English bulldog. For Pete's sake! What did your mother say?"

"She said he looked like Winston Churchill, but she's a Francophile and prefers poodles. Something about Perfidious Albion, whatever that is."

He gave a snort of laughter. "I'll tell you on the way home."

"I have to tell you about Mother, Daddy." And I did. He was not as surprised as I thought he would be. "Did you know? About her drinking, I mean?"

"Yes. It's happened before when you were much younger, usually after you'd gone to bed. I thought maybe she had—but obviously I was wrong. I'm sorry you've had to cope with it." He paused. "I have to tell you, Melissa, I've been in the hospital. That's why—"

"I know," I said. "Miss Pierce told me."

"Oh. Did she?"

We sat in a little silence. After a minute I said, "I like her, even though I didn't think I would."

"I'm glad. She's been a good friend for a long time."

I decided at that moment I didn't want to know any more about it than just that. Not now. And sometime, not now, I would tell her I was sorry I was rude.

"Father, why did you go to the hospital without telling us—well, Mother, anyway?" I couldn't help feeling that if she had known, and not just felt walked out on, she mightn't have drunk, or at least, not as much.

"I didn't actually know I was going to the hospital, Melissa. Oh, I had known for some months that my leg was getting worse. But it was after I left that it acted up."

"But you could have told Mother then."

"Yes. I could. And should. I suppose the unlovely truth is, I was feeling sorry for myself—probably the most unproductive emotion there is. When I was in the hospital I did some thinking—it's a good place for that. And it seemed to me that you had gotten the brunt of all our marital infighting."

"The ball in the ball game," I said, thinking of my conversation with Mother.

"Yes."

"Mother said you had to marry her because she was pregnant with me and that you've always resented it—and me."

"Your mother had no right to tell you that—but who am I to talk? It's a half-truth and half-truths are, or can be, disastrous. Yes, she was pregnant and frightened. But it doesn't follow that I didn't want to marry her. You know, Melissa, we all have our victim fantasies. It's our last consoling resort when things won't go our way. Going to the hospital full of self-pity was mine."

"Sulking." I remembered Miss Ainslie. "Somebody . . . somebody accused me of that recently."

"It doesn't stop automatically when you reach the age to vote. This is your mother's particular victim fantasy. And you can see where it gets her. The world won't do it my way so I'll crawl into the bottle or swallow the pills or get stoned or get myself a fix—or play the misunderstood stoic and withdraw from it all. If I could leave you one thing—more than brains or position or money or even love, I'd leave you the knowledge that you can't take anything for the bumps. You've just got to live through them. They pass. End of lecture. I don't think your mother and I have been very good parents, and the trouble is, it's really too late for that now. I'm sorry, Melissa. You'll have to work harder to find what we forgot to give you. But I think you can do it. You're quite a girl!" He put his arm around me and kissed the top of my head. Then he got up, limped over to the closet and put on his raincoat.

Something made me ask him, "Father, do you really want to go home?"

For a minute he didn't answer. Then he said, "It's not . . . it won't be a permanent arrangement, Melissa. But I can't leave your mother in the present lurch. After all, I helped put her there, and I certainly won't leave you to grapple with it. I have to get some sort of . . . of repair work going before I go into hospital again. But after that—" He looked at me. "There really isn't enough of the marriage to put back together again."

I thought of Mother's "A marriage is a marriage." But what made a marriage? Sadness filled me. Here Father and I were friends really for the first time. But he was right: it was already too late. Because I was I and going in one direction. And they were they, going in another with the problems they would have to work out. And how much longer would I have to share them, anyway? Two years at the most. After that I'd leave home either for college or a job. And if Father decided to stay home now, for good, I'd still leave. So whatever they decided to do had to be for them. Then who would be that mythical person I was always looking for, the one who would tell me what I was supposed to do and be? Miss Ainslie? Joel?

No one. Not even Joel, who would be walking in the same direction. Even with the sadness, it was a relief. And it would be an adventure to find out what I was like, a journey that nobody could take but me.

Father, waiting at the door, was looking anxiously at me. "Do you understand, Melissa? This doesn't have anything to do with you and me. It's not going to change our . . ." he smiled almost shyly, "our new understanding. Is it?"

"No," I said, because I saw he wanted me to, and also because it was true.

"Are you coming, then? To lunch?"

I suddenly realized it would be early when we got home. Joel might be there. And there'd be Hercules waiting for me.

"Yes, coming," I said. I picked up my bag and went through the door ahead of him, just like any other adult-female-lady-woman.

About the Author

Isabelle Holland was born in Basel, Switzerland, where her father was serving as an officer in the American Foreign Service. When she was three, she moved to Guatemala City where, she says, she developed a fondness for things Spanish. After Guatemala, her family moved to northern England where she attended private school, boarding school, and Liverpool University.

Miss Holland never lived in the United States until she was twenty, when her father sent her and her mother home because of the war. She completed college at Tulane University, New Orleans, and then went to New York where she worked in several branches of publishing. She lives in New York City with her cat, Waldo. Miss Holland has written three other books, *Cecily*, *Amanda's Choice*, and *The Man Without a Face*.